THE
PLUM
TREE
WAR

THE
PLUM
TREE
WAR

Bonnie Pryor

ILLUSTRATED BY
Dora Leder

A Yearling Book

Published by
Dell Publishing
a division of
Bantam Doubleday Dell Publishing Group, Inc.
666 Fifth Avenue
New York, New York 10103

Text copyright © 1989 by Bonnie Pryor
Illustrations copyright © 1989 by Dora Leder

The trademark Yearling® is registered in the U.S. Patent and Trademark Office.

The trademark Dell® is registered in the U.S. Patent and Trademark Office.

ISBN: 0-440-40619-6

Reprinted by arrangement with William Morrow and Company, Inc.

Printed in the United States of America

May 1992

10 9 8 7 6 5 4 3 2 1

CWO

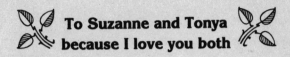 **To Suzanne and Tonya
because I love you both**

 CONTENTS

THE
PLUM TREE WAR

# ONE

Bad News

One Saturday morning in August, Robert Ott's whole life changed. It had been chugging along very smoothly. True, he hadn't even opened the advanced reading text his third-grade teacher had given him to improve his skills. But Robert was sure he'd get to it soon—at least before school started again.

But just past 11:30 the telephone rang, and two pages in the journal his parents had given him for Christmas wouldn't have been enough to list all the problems he had then.

That Saturday Robert's parents were out shopping for new living room furniture. The baby-sitter, Sally Anne, was busy watching cartoons. Robert thought most of the Saturday cartoons were boring, but Sally Anne, who was sixteen and wore gold hoop earrings and purple nail polish, had been sitting in front of the television all morning. Robert had stuck it out until the sight of Sally Anne's fingernails flipping onto the carpet

1

as she clipped them had made him forget his resolve not to let her drive him crazy. He had picked up the nail clippings and thrown them in the trash. It was not a hard job because the purple showed up plainly against the beige carpet.

"They'll come up the next time your mother vacuums," Sally Anne said.

"But they're dirty," Robert exclaimed.

"House dust is mostly human skin cells and hair," Sally Anne said cheerfully. "So I don't think a few fingernails are going to hurt."

Robert cleaned them up anyway. Afterward he sat at the kitchen table to work on the story he was writing. He was debating whether to change the hero to a heroine named Sally Anne, and have her eaten by a dragon who loved the taste of purple nail polish, when the phone rang. It was 11:31. The receiver crackled when Robert picked it up and he knew the call was long distance. He grabbed a paper and pencil from the table by the phone. Robert was very careful about messages.

"Robert, is that you?" his Aunt Frieda asked when he said hello. It took him a few seconds to recognize her voice. Robert explained about the shopping trip.

"Have your mother call me the minute she gets home, will you, sweetie? I might have a nice surprise for you," Aunt Frieda said.

Robert cringed at the "sweetie" but promised he would. He said good-bye politely, wondering what the surprise could be. Aunt Frieda was a climatologist and so was his Uncle John. They taught at a big university in Texas when they weren't traveling around the world studying the effects of weather. Robert knew his mother worried about Aunt Frieda. She was his mother's only sister and Mrs. Ott was afraid that Aunt Frieda might come to harm in some faraway place.

There was a commercial on the television, and Sally Anne wandered into the kitchen. "Was that for me?"

Robert concentrated on writing the message down carefully. *Aunt Frieda called at 11:31. She has a surprise.* Then he answered, "It was for Mom."

Sally Anne twisted the paper to read what he had written.

"You don't have to be that exact." She looked disappointed that the message wasn't for her. A phone call from her boyfriend Jeffrey was the only thing that could drag her away from cartoons on Saturday morning.

"If you are going to do a job, you might as well do it right," Robert said crossly.

"You sure are a grouch this morning." Sally Anne snapped her gum.

Robert couldn't concentrate on his story so he went back to the living room and stared at the television. After a while he smiled at Sally Anne. She wasn't really so bad. She lived three houses up the street from him and he had known her all his life. It wasn't her fault his mom and dad still thought he needed a baby-sitter when he was nine years old and almost ready to start the fourth grade.

Parents were hard to figure out sometimes. On a

4

bright Saturday morning when there was plenty for him to do, they insisted on hiring Sally Anne. But it was different every day after school. Then they had given in to his pleas to let him stay by himself for the thirty minutes until his mother got home from work. Robert's father was a welder at Do-Right Welding Company, and his mother worked as a teacher's aide, but not at Robert's school. At first, they had arranged for Robert to stay with their neighbor, Mrs. Sylvester, until Mrs. Ott came to pick him up. But Robert knew that would be worse than staying alone. Sometimes Mrs. Sylvester annoyed him by peeking out from behind her curtains as if she were spying. And even if she weren't, Robert hated being in her house. Every corner was filled with hundreds of glass miniatures. Sometimes Mrs. Ott took Robert along when Mrs. Sylvester invited her in for coffee. Mrs. Sylvester smiled at Robert and gave him cookies, but she watched him every minute. Robert knew she was worried he would break one of the miniatures. It made him feel like he should sit on the couch with his hands folded tightly in his lap. So Robert had convinced his parents that for such a short time he was old enough to look after himself. He would never admit how much he hated coming home to the cold, empty house.

Robert glanced around the familiar room. The chairs were big and soft and the couch had a comfortable sag. He liked them just the way they were, but Mrs. Ott had announced that she wanted new furniture, without the grape juice and throw-up stains from when Robert was a baby.

"Do you want to play a game of cards or something?" Sally Anne asked.

"No thanks," Robert said. "I guess I'll clean my room."

"You want to clean your room when you don't have to?" Sally Anne looked as though she couldn't believe her ears.

"It's a little messy," Robert explained.

"You are the fussiest person." Sally Anne said it jokingly, but she shook her head as though Robert were an unknown species from the planet X.

Robert went to his room and made his bed. He sat on it—carefully, to keep from messing it up again. He looked with satisfaction at the ship models neatly displayed on his shelves and at his desk with the stories he'd written stacked in their folders. Why did everyone think it was strange that he liked things a certain way? Even Scott and Jason, his best friends at school, teased him sometimes because his desk was always neat and his pencils always sharpened to a perfect point. But they shared his enthusiasm for running. Robert was the fastest runner in the third grade, and maybe in the whole school.

"What kind of furniture did you buy?" Sally Anne asked when Robert's parents came home a short time later.

"Nothing," said Mr. Ott. "Everything we saw was either uncomfortable or too pretty to sit on."

"The few things we did like were too expensive," Mrs. Ott said. She looked around the living room. "Maybe we should re-cover the furniture we've got."

6

"You ought to get some really glamorous antiques," said Sally Anne. "That way your furniture is an investment. My girlfriend Rosalyn's house is filled with them. No one is allowed to sit in her living room because all the furniture is so valuable."

Mr. Ott snorted. "If I am going to spend all that money for furniture, I am certainly not going to sit on the floor."

"By the way, your sister called," Sally Anne told Robert's mother as though she had taken the message.

Mrs. Ott hurried to the spare bedroom. There was a telephone in there, away from the noisy kitchen. "She said she has a surprise," Robert said as his mother dialed.

The conversation was a long one. Sally Anne hung around for as long as she could, obviously hoping to find out about the surprise. Finally she gave up and went home. Robert was dying of curiosity, too, but all he could hear of his mother's conversation were things like "mmmm" and "I see," and even after Mrs. Ott got off the phone she talked to Robert's father for a long time. They shut the bedroom door and Robert couldn't hear a word they were saying, even when he knelt by the connecting heating outlet in his room, which usually carried voices quite well. He had a funny feeling something awful was about to happen.

At last his parents returned to the living room. By that time Robert had given up trying to listen and was working on the one-thousand-piece puzzle Aunt Frieda and Uncle John had sent him for his birthday in June. He was still only half done.

"I have some news for you," said Mrs. Ott. "Aunt Frieda and Uncle John have been asked to join a team of scientists in Antarctica."

Robert looked up in amazement. Antarctica was the South Pole.

"But of course they can't take your cousin, Harriet. So she is going to stay with us for the school year."

"Here?" Robert asked. "In our house?"

"Of course," laughed Mr. Ott. "Did you think we would build her an apartment in the yard?"

Robert could hardly believe his ears. Here he was worried about changing furniture and it was his whole life that was going to change.

"It might be nice for you," said Mrs. Ott. "You and Harriet are the same age, after all."

Robert sighed. Harriet might be the same age, but he hardly knew her. It had been a year since Aunt Frieda and Uncle John had visited, and all he could remember about Harriet was that she was always bragging about how great it was in Texas. His life was perfect just the way it was, and he certainly didn't want a girl who was practically a stranger coming in and changing it. Even new furniture that no one could sit on would be better than that.

TWO

Harri and the Monster

A few days later Robert sat in the crook of his favorite tree. He was trying, without much success, to concentrate on a large, colorfully illustrated textbook. It was filled with reading selections, a list of questions and exercises following each one. Mrs. Shoemaker, his teacher from last year, had given it to him. She said that if he worked hard over the summer, he might make it into the highest reading group in the fourth grade. He had tried all through the third grade but never succeeded. It wasn't that he couldn't read as well as his friends. But every time he started to read, his mind wanted to think about other things.

"You have a wonderful imagination," Mrs. Shoemaker had told him. "But you have to learn when to let it run free and when to work."

Robert put his finger in the book and closed it. He sighed. The old plum tree was a wonderful place to sit. It had been his special place for as long as he could remember. Even when he was too little to climb the tree by himself he had asked his father to lift him up into its branches. Two of the biggest branches came out at just the right angle to make a comfortable place to sit. From there he could look over the wooded ravine that ran behind all the yards on Greenwell Street. By mutual agreement, none of the neighbors fenced the woods, and for most of the year it was a wonderful place to walk, although in the summer it was overrun with weeds and vines. The woods were home to many small animals. Robert had seen squirrels and chipmunks, rabbits, and pesky raccoons that sometimes picked off the lids of garbage cans in the neighborhood and dumped them over looking for food. Once or twice, Robert had even seen a deer.

He loved the woods, but his favorite spot was still the plum tree. In the spring the tree was covered with fragrant blossoms, and later in the summer there were huge plums. They were a dusty color, but when rubbed they would turn bright purple. Robert picked one from the branch above his head and took a juicy bite. He looked at the book, but he didn't open it. The trouble was that the stories in the book were boring. He suspected he could write more interesting stories himself. Last year he had written one about a wild horse. Mrs. Shoemaker had hung it in the hall so everyone could read it. His current story, about the dinosaur who almost ate Sally Anne, had short chapters and was terribly exciting. He wanted to have it done when school started, but with Harriet coming he wondered if he would have time.

A bluebird landed on a branch near him and Robert smiled. The bird and its mate had built a nest in the Otts' backyard, in a birdhouse Robert and his father had placed high on a post. Robert had helped his father make the house, measuring carefully so that the hole was just the right size.

"What would happen if the hole wasn't right?" Robert had asked.

Mr. Ott showed him a picture of two bluebirds. They were a pretty blue color and the male had a red breast like a robin. "There used to be a lot of bluebirds in Ohio," Mr. Ott explained. "But other birds, like the starling, steal their nesting places and kill their babies. So a lot of people are trying to help the bluebirds by building houses with entrance holes big enough for the bluebirds, but too little for the starlings."

"I wonder why the starlings are so mean?" said Robert.

"They're not really mean," said Mr. Ott. "They weren't any problem in England, where they lived. But well-meaning people brought them to America because they liked the way they sang. They multiplied like crazy. Now in most areas they are quite a problem, driving out the natural population of other birds. That's what happens when you tamper with old Mother Nature." His father had grinned. "But we are going to give Mother Nature a hand."

Robert watched the bluebirds. He knew there were four pale blue eggs in the nest. It was late in the summer for hatching, but bluebirds sometimes raised several batches of babies a year. It would be fun to watch

11

them when they started to fly. It made him feel good to know he had helped.

He noticed Mrs. Sylvester peering up suspiciously from her yard. "What do you do in that tree all day?" she said. "A boy your age should be doing something useful."

Robert sighed, his peaceful mood broken. "I'm reading a book," he said.

"I suppose I shouldn't complain. At least you aren't running around making noise and breaking windows." She looked thoughtful for a minute. "I need someone to clean my garage. Would you like the job? I'll pay you."

Cleaning Mrs. Sylvester's garage was the last thing Robert wanted to do, but he didn't know how to refuse politely.

"I guess I could," he said. "But not today. My Aunt Frieda is coming with my cousin Harriet."

Mrs. Sylvester peered up into the tree again. "Oh, really," she said, curiosity gleaming in her eyes. "Is she the archaeologist? Why is she coming?"

"She's a climatologist," Robert corrected. He wished Mrs. Sylvester would leave him alone. "Harriet is going to stay with us while my aunt and uncle go to Antarctica."

"I'd love to meet your aunt. You tell your mother to bring her over and introduce her. You hear, Robbie?"

Robert winced at the hated nickname. "I will, Mrs. Sylvester," he said, trying to sound pleasant. Mrs. Sylvester shuffled away and Robert looked through the leaves at the sky, filled with puffy shapes. There was a cloud that looked like a horse, rearing up as if in fear or anger. No wonder. Right in front of it was the terrible lizard, *Tyrannosaurus rex.* There were three smaller clouds. From where he sat they looked like three duck-billed dinosaurs sitting right on top of his house. Robert blinked. There was a strange car and the sound of a familiar voice—Aunt Frieda's. She must have arrived early, while he'd been daydreaming. He sighed. His mother had promised he could help bake cookies, and now there wouldn't be time.

He poked the last of the plum into his mouth and started to swing down from the tree. But just as he did he saw a giant black creature charging across the lawn, heading right toward the tree.

For one wild second Robert thought it was a bear. But then he realized that it was a dog, the biggest dog he had ever seen, and furthermore it was making loud, unfriendly noises. There was a girl running right behind it. The last time he had seen Harriet she had short hair. Now she had long blond braids and she was taller, but Robert didn't have time to think about how much she'd changed. Every time the dog barked he could see its sharp white fangs.

Robert tried to scramble back up the tree, but he was hindered by the book and couldn't get a good grip. Frantically he swung his legs up, wrapping them around a branch. There he hung, legs around one branch, arms around another, and his rear end hanging down handy for the dog to take a bite.

"Monster," Harriet shouted. "Behave yourself."

Robert moaned and closed his eyes. Monster? He

could almost feel those teeth sinking into his jeans. There would probably be a lot of blood. And how was he going to sit down when school started next week? That is, if he was even alive to worry about it.

Suddenly he realized that everything was quiet. Too quiet. He forced himself to open his eyes.

The dog was sitting quietly beneath the tree. His head was cocked sideways and he was giving Robert a quizzical look, as though trying to understand why he was in such a strange position. Harriet was standing beside the dog, her head also tilted to one side. She was grinning widely.

"Is that some kind of strange new exercise?" she asked.

Robert felt his face growing hot as he realized how stupid he must look. He was still not sure about the dog. He looked peaceful now, but what might he do if Robert climbed down? The dog was big enough to have two Roberts for a mid-morning snack.

"Get that dog away," Robert yelled, sputtering with embarrassment.

"Monster? He won't hurt you. He is really gentle."

"If he is so gentle, why do you call him Monster?"

"That's what Frieda calls him. 'Get that Monster out of the house.'" Harriet did a perfect imitation of her mother's voice.

For a minute Robert forgot his fear. "You call your mom by her name?"

"Why not? It's kind of boring calling your parents Mom and Dad, just like everyone else. Let's say you were lost in a crowd. If you yelled *Mom,* you might be trampled by a hundred moms all coming to rescue you."

Robert paused to digest this rather startling statement. In a weird way it made a lot of sense.

"Do you need any help?" Harriet asked. "You look pretty stupid hanging there like a monkey."

Robert dropped his legs to the ground, but he lost his grip and tumbled down into a heap. Instantly Monster was on him, smothering him with slobbery kisses. "Harriet, get him *away!*" Robert yelled.

Harriet pulled the dog away long enough for Robert to stand up. "Most of my friends call me Harri," she informed him. "Do you like to be called Bobby or Robbie?"

"Robert," he said in a grumpy voice as he brushed the dirt from his clothes and checked his skinned elbow.

"That's so *stuffy,*" Harri said, making a face.

"Well, Harry's pretty dumb," Robert retorted. "It's a boy's name."

"Do I look like a boy?" Harri asked. "Besides, I spell it with an *i*. She spotted the book Robert was trying to hide. "Hey, we had to read that book last year. Didn't you?"

Robert shrugged. "No."

"Why read such a boring book over the *summer?*"

"I wish I didn't have to," Robert confessed. "But if I finish it before fourth grade, I might get put in the highest reading group this year."

"I'm always in the highest reading group. What a great spot." Harriet was looking at the plum tree. "It's

16

so private. We ought to form a club and have our meetings right here. I'll make up the rules and pick a really good name," she added.

Even if Robert did want to make a club, which he didn't, that didn't seem fair. "Why should you get to make up all the rules?"

"Because I thought of the idea first. And anyway, I know all about clubs," Harri answered. "I was the president of the best club in my whole school. Everyone wanted to join. We had secret passwords," she added, as though that explained the club's popularity.

Robert only half-listened to Harri's ideas as they walked back to the house. He was thinking about bluebirds and starlings. He was the bluebird, he thought, just minding his own business and not bothering anyone. Harri was the starling. Maybe she was all right where she belonged, but she was a pest in Ohio. How was he going to stand a whole year with her? They had only spent five minutes together and already there were three things about Harri he didn't like. She was a better reader than he was, she had a horrible dog, and she was just too bossy.

THREE

Monsters and Bony Knees

Dinner that night was a festive occasion, at least for the adults. Robert helped himself to roast beef, potatoes, and green beans, carefully arranging the food on his plate so that nothing touched. Robert looked at Harri's plate and shuddered to see her green beans covered with gravy. Robert never let one kind of food touch another. One day Mr. Ott had noticed how carefully Robert dished up his food. "It all goes together in your stomach," he said cheerfully. After that Robert remembered to eat everything in order. If he ate his meat and waited a few seconds before starting on his potatoes, he reasoned, they would not get so mixed up in his stomach.

Robert started on his roast beef. Monster had been shut in the screened front porch, a fact that relieved Robert but made Harri very unhappy.

"When are you going back?" Mr. Ott asked Aunt Frieda.

"Tomorrow morning, early." Aunt Frieda sighed. "John is making the arrangements. We will only have two days to pack before we're scheduled to leave."

To Robert, Aunt Frieda didn't look like a lady who spent half her time tramping around the Earth. If anything, she looked like Robert's no-nonsense second-grade teacher. It was hard to believe that she and his mother were sisters. Aunt Frieda was tall and thin, while his mother was short and round. Aunt Frieda wore her hair severely pulled back, as if to show that she had better things to do than fool around with her looks. Her speech was quick and sharp, like the rest of her, and she didn't smile very often. Her knees were so bony that it was hard for Robert to imagine being a baby and sitting on her lap. Still, there was something similar about Aunt Frieda and his mother. He studied them awhile before he decided that both of them had the same gray eyes and the same tiny wrinkles around the corners. Harri's eyes were like theirs, but without the wrinkles.

"I hope Monster is not a problem," Aunt Frieda said. "Harri couldn't bear to give him away, and it seemed cruel to board him in a kennel for a year."

"He's a little bigger than I imagined," Mrs. Ott said. "But I think we can manage." Robert thought she sounded awfully calm for a lady with a monster right outside her door.

"Why don't you tell Harri about your school?" Mr. Ott urged Robert.

He had been so busy thinking about Aunt Frieda that the question startled Robert. He wondered what

19

he should tell her. "Well," he stammered. "It's called Elmwood. There are about three hundred kids."

"My old school has eight hundred," Harri said quickly. "It has air conditioning and a swimming pool."

"Well, we don't need air conditioning year-round in Ohio," Mrs. Ott pointed out. "Elmwood is a nice little school."

"There are two fourth grades," Robert said. He crossed his fingers under the table, hoping he and Harri would be in different classrooms.

"Is there a track team?" Harri interrupted. "I'm on the track team at home. I've won four blue ribbons."

"Robert loves to run, too," said Mr. Ott. "But you'd have to be in sixth grade to qualify for the track team."

Harri's mouth had set in a thin, straight line.

"Has Harri told you the reason for our expedition, Robert?" Aunt Frieda asked quickly.

Robert shook his head.

"Some scientists, and your Uncle John and I are among them, believe that the Earth is growing warmer because of pollution. You've probably heard it called the greenhouse effect. The potential of such a change could be very serious, particularly if the polar ice caps began to melt."

Robert must have looked alarmed, because Aunt Frieda smiled and said encouragingly, "There's plenty we can do to help reverse this process, but we have to understand it first. We are going to Antarctica to study a hole in the part of the atmosphere called the ozone layer to see if it's part of the problem. We

20

wouldn't leave Harri like this if we didn't feel our work was so crucial." She patted Harri's hand.

"I feel so much better, Harri, knowing that Robert will be here to help you make friends." When Harri didn't respond she went on. "And Christmas will be here before you know it."

"I don't need anybody to help me," Harri suddenly burst out. She jumped up from her chair so quickly that it almost tipped over. "Can I be excused?" She hurried from the dining room without waiting for an answer.

Nobody spoke.

Aunt Frieda looked distressed. "I must apologize for Harri," she finally said. "She's looking forward to staying with you. I know she is. And after all, we'll be together at Christmas."

Robert poked the last green bean into his mouth and swallowed quickly without chewing. That way he didn't have to taste it.

"Don't worry," said Mrs. Ott. "I have a lot of things planned. It will be nice having a girl in the house."

Robert scowled at his mother. How could she say such a thing? She sounded as if she really meant it.

His mother didn't seem to notice Robert's expression. "Why don't you help Harri unpack?" she said. "One of her suitcases is still in the hall."

"We'll all see that Harri feels at home," Mr. Ott said to Aunt Frieda, giving Robert a warning look.

"I'm going to decorate the guest room so that it will feel more like a girl's room," Mrs. Ott reassured her. "Harri can help me."

Robert went reluctantly to retrieve the suitcase. He carried it to the guest room, glancing around it as he pushed open the door. He liked this room. The walls were painted yellow and the bedspread and curtains had a soft floral design that reminded him of spring. Sometimes in the winter he came here to sit and it always made him feel warmer. He didn't understand why his mother thought it needed redecorating.

Harri gave him a sour look. "Don't you know how to knock?" She was holding a stuffed monkey, which she hastily shoved into a dresser drawer.

"Sorry," Robert said, setting down the heavy suitcase. "I didn't think about it." He knew he should have knocked, but it made him feel strange to know that now there was a part of his house he couldn't enter when he wanted.

"My room at home is much bigger," she said, "and I have a canopy bed."

"This is a nice room," Robert said.

"I didn't say it wasn't," Harri said crossly. "I just said my room at home is bigger."

Carefully, Robert started to remove Harri's clothes from the suitcase, not sure exactly what he should do. Harri pushed him aside, pulled at handfuls of clothing, and stuffed them into the dresser drawers. Robert sat down in the rocking chair and watched. The chair was an old one he and his father had found one day at an auction. They had brought it home and Robert had helped his father strip and refinish it. They had rubbed it until it gleamed like new.

"How do you like this chair?" he asked. He couldn't think of anything else to say.

Harri shrugged. "It's okay, I guess. I like modern furniture. In our house everything is too old and musty. When I have my own house I want everything new."

"Shouldn't you fold those things when you put them in the drawer?" Robert asked, trying to hide his hurt feelings.

Harri looked genuinely puzzled. "Why go to all that work? I'm just going to take them out and wear them."

She reached into her pocket and pulled out several pieces of roast beef from dinner. She put them on the nightstand. "I saved these for Monster," she explained. "I always give him treats from dinner."

"He is awfully big," Robert said. "I'm surprised Aunt Frieda let you bring him."

"I screamed," Harri said mildly. "Frieda can't stand it. She always gives me what I want if I scream. If that doesn't work, I hold my breath until I turn blue. That really works."

Robert was shocked. "It wouldn't work with my parents."

Harri shrugged. "It might. The trick is not to do it very often. Only when it is something really important." Her gray eyes suddenly looked very dark and fierce. "Monster is very important. He loves me."

Harri continued unpacking her suitcase in a matter-of-fact way, as though she had not said anything unusual. Robert sighed and wished he could escape. Surely his mother didn't expect him to help Harri put away embarrassing things like underwear.

23

"This place is the pits," Harri said. "I'll bet you hate it living in such a little town."

"N-no," Robert stammered in surprise. "Why would I hate it?"

Harri waved her arm. "Oh, I don't mean the house. It's okay, I guess. But I much prefer the city. There are so many cultural advantages. In Dallas where we live there are museums and art galleries, things like that. And sometimes I get to travel with my parents. We went to Africa for three months last year. We took some trips into places that were really primitive, but we stayed in a big modern city."

Robert thought about Mount Stanton. It was a pleasant little town with clean streets and shady trees. Even downtown the streets were lined with pink and white crab apple trees. In the spring, the whole town seemed like one giant flower show. Maybe it wasn't as exciting as Africa, but it was a good place.

"I like it here," Robert said.

Harri gave him a pitying look as if to say he was too dumb to know better. "That figures." She shrugged. "Boring town. Boring person. I suppose Monster will like it. He's never had a chance to walk in the woods."

Robert felt his mouth drop open. He might be boring, but Harri was the rudest person he had ever met.

"If you like Dallas so much," he said, his heart pounding hard, "it's too bad you couldn't stay there."

"My parents' work is very important," Harri said. "You probably wouldn't even be able to understand it. They make a lot of sacrifices for their work and so do

24

I." She threw Robert a challenging look and dumped the contents of the suitcase on her bed.

Robert's face was bright red, and only the memory of his father's warning look kept him sitting in the rocker.

Harri was stuffing some pink flowered underwear into a drawer and Robert looked up at the ceiling, pretending not to notice. In the corner there was a tiny spider, spinning a web. He pressed his lips shut and didn't say a word. Maybe it would drop down on her head during the night. He went out and slammed the door.

The grown-ups were all in the living room talking. Robert grabbed his journal and slipped out the kitchen door. Monster was on the front porch, so at least he didn't have to walk past him. It was cool outside and Robert realized sadly that summer was almost over. School would start in a few days. He headed for the plum tree with a piece of bread he had taken from the kitchen breadbox. Early in the summer he had seen two red squirrels at the edge of the woods. He had named them Red and Nutty. It had taken him all summer to win their trust. Every night he brought them a treat. He would sit without moving a muscle, each time placing the bread a little nearer, until now the squirrels would come up really close. Usually they were waiting for him at the edge of the woods, but tonight there was no sign of them. Robert wrote in his journal while he waited. Sometimes it was hard to talk about things that bothered him, but if he wrote them down it always made him feel better. This time he made a list. Across the top of the page he wrote as neatly as he could, *Things I Hate.* Under it he wrote:

> purple nail polish
> girls' underwear
> boring books
> big mean dogs
> Harri

"You shouldn't feed those greedy pests," Mrs. Sylvester called from her yard. "Every time I put out seed for the birds they steal it. Feeding just encourages them to come around."

"I like them," Robert said. Sometimes he felt like being really awful to Mrs. Sylvester. But his mother and father had made him promise to be polite. "She's just lonely," Mrs. Ott had said. "She means well, but she's not used to children."

"In my day children spoke respectfully to their elders and listened when they tried to teach them something," Mrs. Sylvester said.

"I just said I liked squirrels," Robert answered.

Mrs. Sylvester turned toward her house. But she had only taken three steps when she turned around again. "Who does that horrible dog belong to?"

Robert explained. "Well," Mrs. Sylvester said in a grouchy voice, "I certainly hope your parents keep him tied up. I don't want him over here trampling on my flowers."

Robert didn't like Monster either, but Mrs. Sylvester

was making him mad. Her flowers were just a few ragged marigolds in a patch by her back door.

"He won't bother your flowers," he answered curtly. Then he was ashamed. Mrs. Sylvester had arthritis in her hands and he knew it was hard for her to garden. "I'll clean the garage tomorrow," he called after her politely.

Mrs. Sylvester made a noise that sounded like *Hrumpfh.* "I'll expect you in the morning. And you'll have to do a good job if you want to be paid." With that she marched back to her house.

It was on the tip of his tongue to yell after her that he had changed his mind, that no one else would work for her because she was so mean. But he bit back the words and opened his journal. He added "nosy neighbors" to his list. Robert leaned back against the tree with a sigh. There was still no sign of Nutty and Red. He had just defended Monster to Mrs. Sylvester, but he knew Monster was to blame for Red and Nutty's reluctance to leave the safety of the woods. It wasn't even Monster's fault. It was just one more thing Harri had ruined by coming.

# FOUR

Roller Coasters and an Argument

Robert's gloomy mood didn't improve the next morning. He snapped off his night-light, a comforting carry-over from toddler days, stumbled to the bathroom, and reached for his toothbrush. Then he froze. The toothbrush in his hand was green, and his own blue brush was hanging on the wrong side of the holder. After he brushed his teeth, he moved his toothbrush back to its regular spot and eyed the bathroom glass suspiciously. It was probably covered with Harri's germs. His parents always used the small bathroom that opened off their bedroom, leaving the hall bathroom to him. Now it seemed he was going to have to share it.

He dressed and went to the kitchen, where he got another unpleasant surprise. There was Harri, stuffing her mouth with waffles, sitting in his chair.

"That's my chair," he said.

Harri made no effort to move. "Now, Robert," Mrs.

Ott said reasonably. "It doesn't really make any difference where you sit."

"It does to me," Robert said. "I always sit there."

Harri still did not move, and finally Robert slid into the other chair. "Where is Aunt Frieda?" he asked.

"She left very early," Mrs. Ott said.

Harri jabbed her fork into a piece of waffle and her eyes brimmed with tears. Mr. Ott cleared his throat.

"I have a great idea." He looked from one downcast face to the other. "This is the last week we'll have a chance to go to Pirate's Point. Would anyone be interested in a little trip?"

"What's Pirate's Point?" Harri wiped her eyes on the back of her hand.

"It's an amusement park," Robert told her, feeling a little more sympathetic. He could imagine how terrible it would be if he had to spend the school year with Aunt Frieda and Uncle John in Texas. His father had planned this outing as a surprise to cheer up Harri. Robert was feeling more cheerful, too.

It was, after all, Robert's favorite breakfast. In the Ott household Mr. Ott was the breakfast cook. He was a morning person, while Mrs. Ott liked to stay in bed until the last minute. You could always tell what day it was by what Mr. Ott fixed for breakfast. Mondays and Thursdays were cold cereal, Tuesdays and Fridays were hot cereal. Wednesdays and Saturdays were eggs, and Sundays were pancakes. Waffles and bacon were a special treat because Mr. Ott did not like to clean the waffle iron. Robert happily forked up his share. To

29

top it off, the weather was perfect. Summer weather in Ohio was often hot and muggy, but today was just right.

"But what about work?" Robert asked. Mrs. Ott was off all summer, but Robert's father had already taken his vacation when they went to the beach earlier in the summer. He did not miss work often.

"Things are a little slow at work right now," Mr. Ott said. "They won't mind my taking a day off. As a matter of fact, I'll call right now, and just as soon as you finish breakfast we'll take off."

"Whoopee," yelled Robert, stuffing the last forkful into his mouth. Harri smiled, but she didn't look very excited.

"It's great," he told her. "We went there last summer. There are all kinds of rides. You'll love it."

"Frieda and John take me to amusement parks all the time. Texas has some really great ones. What kind of rides does Pirate's Point have?"

"Merry-go-rounds, bumper cars, train rides—everything," Robert said, refusing to let Harri's bragging spoil his day.

"Roller coasters?"

"Three of them," Mrs. Ott said. "But let's quit talking about it and go see for ourselves."

"I want to go on the biggest roller coaster," Harri announced. Robert felt his stomach do a tiny flip-flop. He liked most of the rides at the park. But he had never been on a roller coaster, and he never wanted to. They looked awful. The one at Pirate's Point even turned upside down. Just thinking about it made him feel like throwing up.

He forgot about the roller coaster once they were on the highway headed for the park. It was going to be a wonderful day. With luck his parents would agree to stay for the nightly fireworks display.

By the time Mr. Ott maneuvered the car into a parking space, even Harri was looking more cheerful. The parking lot was huge and it was filled with thousands of cars. There were little trolley buses whisking people to the gates. "Let's ride the roller coaster first thing," Harri said when they were seated on the trolley.

"The best one is on the other side of the park," Mrs. Ott said, giving Robert a sympathetic look. She understood how he felt about roller coasters. "Let's just look at things as we walk along. If we start dashing all over the park, we'll get too tired."

Costumed characters were walking around greeting people. A marching band flashed by. Inside the tiny shops that filled one section there were all kinds of weird things for sale. The family headed straight for the dolphin act, which was just starting. They found seats in the very first row, and when the dolphin jumped through a hoop, Robert got splashed.

They stopped at a refreshment stand and bought hot dogs, eating them at a little table beneath a striped umbrella. At home, Robert didn't really like hot dogs. But for some reason hot dogs tasted heavenly at the amusement park.

Harri pointed to the roller coaster that was towering above the umbrella. "Can we go on it next, Margaret?" she asked.

Mrs. Ott looked startled at the use of her first name, but she recovered quickly.

"I'm not sure you should go so soon after lunch," she said.

"She's right," said Robert quickly. "It might make us sick, going upside down."

Harri gave him a shrewd look. "You aren't afraid, are you?"

"Of course not," Robert said crossly. "I just like some of the other rides better."

Mrs. Ott didn't like roller coasters, either. "Why don't you go with Uncle Fred, Harri? Robert and I will find something else," she said.

Mrs. Ott had said *Uncle* Fred very pointedly, but if Harri noticed she ignored it. "How about it, Fred?" she asked.

"I'm not sure I'm up to the roller coaster," Mr. Ott said. "Getting old, I guess."

"Come on, Robert. Ride with me," Harri coaxed.

Robert gulped. Suddenly the day wasn't so wonderful. Why didn't Harri just shut up about roller coasters? Now he was trapped. If he didn't go, she would know he was afraid.

There was a long line at the ride. "Look how long we will have to wait," he said, hoping Harri would change her mind. But Harri shrugged happily.

"They're moving pretty fast. It won't be that long."

33

"You don't have to go if you don't want to, Robert," said Mrs. Ott.

"No, I want to go," Robert said without enthusiasm. He got in line with Harri while his parents waited on a bench nearby.

"This is going to be so much fun," Harri squealed. "Of course the ones at home are bigger, but this is pretty nice."

"Bigger?" Robert stared at the giant ride as the line slowly moved up a ramp. He felt his hands sweating. What if he fell out or had a heart attack? Even worse, what if he screamed like a baby?

By the time they reached the platform and got a seat in the little train, Robert was already sick to his stomach. He knew he would never get through the ride without throwing up. He thought of all the poor people walking under the roller coaster who would get splashed with half-digested hot dogs. The thought made him moan.

Harri grinned wickedly. "You look kind of pale. Are you sure you're not scared?"

Robert didn't even answer. The train was starting to move. Up, up, the wheels went *clickity-clack* as the train climbed to the top of the first big curve. Robert gripped the bar in front of him until his knuckles were white. He forgot about Harri. He forgot about everything except trying not to scream.

There was an instant when they seemed suspended high above the amusement park. Robert thought he saw his mother and father like tiny ants below him. Then the train teetered over the edge and they were thundering straight down. Robert was slammed back against the seat, and the wind roared past his face. The cars swooped through the bottom of the curve and started up again, but Robert's stomach seemed to be several seconds behind. When it caught up to his body he felt a sickening lurch. The train was already at the top of the second incline, this one even bigger than the first. But he was ready. It wasn't so terrible after all. In fact, he was actually having fun. It was a great feeling, Robert realized, almost like flying. He turned to smile at Harri.

But Harri was not smiling and her face was so pale it looked as if she was about to cry. "I hate this," she screamed as the train started down again. This was the loop where they went upside down. "Let me off, let me off," screamed Harri. Her face looked wild and she grabbed at Robert's shirt, almost tearing it. Robert reached over and held her hand just as they were suddenly turned upside down. Harri closed her eyes and kept screaming. She didn't stop even though the next few chutes were not as steep.

When the train rolled at last to a stop, they staggered off. Harri's face was tearstained and she gulped to keep from throwing up. Robert felt sorry for her but he couldn't help grinning.

"That was great," he said. "I thought I would hate it but it was wonderful." He smiled understandingly at Harri. "I'm sorry you didn't like it."

"Show-off," Harri whispered loudly. "Don't you dare tell anyone. I wasn't really afraid. I just went on too soon after we ate."

Robert stared at her in disbelief. "Look who's calling someone a show-off. That's all you ever do. You're the one who has been bragging about riding roller coasters all day. I didn't even want to go."

"You think you are so perfect, don't you, *Robbie*," she whispered furiously. "You are nothing but a stuck-up baby who has to sleep with a light."

Robert recoiled. He'd always slept with his night-light on that was shaped like a tiny sailboat. "Well, *you* are a spoiled brat," he yelled, embarrassed that she knew his secret. Harri burst into tears and ran to Mrs. Ott.

"Oh, honey, I thought you liked roller coasters," Mrs. Ott said, handing her a tissue. "Robert doesn't really like them, either."

"It's not because of the roller coaster," Harri lied. "Robert was calling me names."

Mr. Ott gave Robert a disapproving look. "Is that true?"

"I said she was a spoiled brat, but she—"

"I'm disappointed in you, Robert," Mr. Ott interrupted. "This is Harri's first day here. I expected you to act like a gentleman."

Harri's look from behind the tissue was triumphant. She pulled Mrs. Ott over to watch some tumbling clowns. Robert followed and stood without smiling. Even clowns couldn't make the day bright again.

FIVE

A Ship in a Bottle

It had been almost midnight when the family arrived home. Robert slept late the next morning, worn out from the excitement. The day at Pirate's Point had ended happily after all. Robert had ridden the roller coaster two more times, once with his dad and once alone. Harri had refused to get on again, but there had been plenty of other rides. They had stayed until the dazzling fireworks display signaled the park was about to close.

Robert stretched and yawned. There was a warm spicy smell in his room, which meant his mother was already up and baking cookies. Robert sat bolt upright in bed. He always helped his mother bake cookies. Would she have started without him? He jumped into his clothes and ran straight to the kitchen, then stood in the doorway trying to swallow his anger. It was obvious why his mother hadn't waited.

Usually, baking cookies was a special time for Robert

and his mother. While the cookies baked they would have a long talk over hot cocoa, or an icy lemonade if it was hot. But today Harri was in the kitchen, giggling with Mrs. Ott over some adventure with lost suitcases. Mrs. Ott laughed. It sounded to Robert like she was really enjoying Harri's company. Maybe she really did wish she'd had a girl of her own.

"Mrs. Sylvester wants me to clean out her garage," Robert said.

His mother looked up from the cookies. "Do a good job for her," she said absently.

He had hoped his mother might say something nice like "How wonderful," or "I'm proud of you," but Mrs. Ott went right on chatting with Harri. Robert gobbled down his breakfast and went out the door. Monster was sitting in the shade of the Otts' garage, tied to a long rope. He jumped up and whined, but Robert made a wide circle around him. Monster looked disappointed. He's probably sorry he can't take a bite out of my arm, Robert thought grimly.

It was a miserably hot and humid day, not the right kind of day for cleaning out garages. He consoled himself with the thought of the money he would earn. He'd been saving all summer for a special ship-in-a-bottle kit at the hobby shop downtown, adding to his birthday money by doing odd jobs around the house. The kit was for a big double-masted sailing ship, and according to the advertising on the box—*Easy-to-follow directions inside*—anyone could make it. Robert knew exactly what the box said because he had looked at it so many times. But the kit cost $19.95

and Robert only had sixteen dollars. He knew Mrs. Sylvester's garage was a mess, because he had peeked inside the open door on one of the rare occasions when Mrs. Sylvester drove to town. If he did a really super job, maybe she would give him five dollars. That would be enough to buy the kit at last.

Sally Anne was riding her bike past his house as he walked around to the front yard. She waved and stopped. "Did you get your aunt's surprise?"

"It wasn't a surprise. It was a curse," Robert told her. "My cousin is staying for the whole school year."

"That doesn't sound so bad. It might be nice having someone for company."

"My cousin is a girl. And she's just taking over everything." Robert kicked a rock so hard it hurt his toe.

"Well, maybe it will get better," Sally Anne said sympathetically. "My sisters and brother are pains, too, but I'd be lonely without them. I'm going to the store. Why don't you get your bike and come with me?"

"I can't," Robert said. "I promised to clean Mrs. Sylvester's garage."

"Jeffrey did it yesterday afternoon," Sally Anne said. "I think he's earning some money to take me somewhere special."

Robert was sure he had misunderstood her. "Mrs. Sylvester asked me, not Jeffrey," he said, not sure he believed his ears. "I was supposed to do it yesterday morning but we went to Pirate's Point."

Sally Anne shrugged. "Maybe she was tired of waiting. Are you coming or not?"

"I guess not," Robert said glumly. "I'd better go talk to Mrs. Sylvester."

"Suit yourself," Sally Anne said. She waved as she rode off.

Robert crossed the yard and knocked on Mrs. Sylvester's door. He was certain Sally Anne had misunderstood.

Mrs. Sylvester opened the door a tiny crack and peeked through. "What is it?"

"Your garage," Robert explained. "You wanted me to clean it."

"Already done," Mrs. Sylvester said. "I thought you weren't coming. Gave the job to Jeffrey up the street." She leaned down and shook her finger. "Let that be a lesson for you. The early bird catches the worm."

Robert sighed as he turned to go home. "I don't suppose a boy your age needs money for anything very important," the old woman called after him. "Probably would have just spent it on candy."

"I am too saving for something special," Robert answered. He told her about the ship-in-a-bottle kit.

"A ship in a bottle, eh? My father used to build them. Only he didn't use any kit. Built them right from scratch. Got a few of them in the house. Want to see?"

Robert hesitated, but his curiosity was stronger than his reluctance to enter the house. He nodded and stepped inside.

The house had a musty smell Robert hated. Each room was cluttered with knickknacks, and shelves filled with the glass figurines were everywhere. Robert walked carefully as he followed Mrs. Sylvester to the back of the house. He wished he had gone straight home, until Mrs. Sylvester opened a bedroom door and motioned him inside.

The furniture in the room was old and dusty, as though no one went in there very often. But it was the ships that caught his eye. There were dozens of them, all kinds, displayed on shelves and practically every surface. The one sitting on the dresser made him gasp with delight—a magnificent pirate ship encased in a bottle. "It's wonderful," Robert said, almost forgetting to breathe.

Mrs. Sylvester beamed, and the usual frown lines around her mouth relaxed. "That's my favorite, too. I can remember my dad sitting at our kitchen table at night working on it. Didn't have electricity in those days, just a smoky old lantern. But my dad would sit there for hours. He was born by the sea. Came to Ohio and became a farmer, but never stopped missing it. Took him almost two years to finish this one."

Robert peered through the glass at the perfect details of the model ship. The sails billowed in an imaginary breeze and tiny figures swaggered about the deck. A skull and crossbones was emblazoned on the jaunty flag.

"Thank you for showing it to me," said Robert. He had a sudden image of Mrs. Sylvester as a little girl, leaning on her elbows on a table, watching her father make ships in bottles by the dim light of an oil lamp. "I'd never be able to build one that good."

"I doubt if my father's first ship was all that fine," Mrs. Sylvester said dryly. "But he kept trying." Her voice

41

softened. "I'll tell you what. My hedges along the side of the yard need trimming. If you would like the job, maybe I can help you get that ship."

Robert worked all morning, cutting the hedges carefully to make them even and straight. It was hot and the clippers made blisters on his palms, but a vision of the ship-in-a-bottle kit kept him going.

Harri came outside and romped with Monster in the Otts' yard. Robert was half finished and she came over to watch. Monster squeezed through the bushes and sniffed around Mrs. Sylvester's back door.

"You get that dog out of my yard, Missy," Mrs. Sylvester called, opening the door a crack. Robert wondered if she had been watching all along.

"Monster's not hurting anything," Harri said. "And my name is not Missy."

"Whatever your name is, you get your dog out of here or I'll call the dogcatcher," Mrs. Sylvester yelled.

"All right," Harri said. She grabbed Monster's collar. "Grouchy old bag," she muttered under her breath, but loudly enough for Mrs. Sylvester to hear.

"Sassy little thing, aren't you?" Mrs. Sylvester said, opening her door wider. "You could learn a few things from your cousin here. At least he knows how to be polite."

Robert felt himself blushing. He was surprised because Mrs. Sylvester sounded as if she actually liked him a little. Maybe it was because they both loved model ships. But as Harri flounced by, dragging Monster, she shouted, "Who'd want to be like him?"

Mrs. Sylvester disappeared inside her house. Robert

43

worked furiously, hoping she wouldn't blame him for Harri's rude behavior. At last he was finished. Somewhat timidly he knocked on the back door.

"You did a nice job," said Mrs. Sylvester. Her voice sounded almost friendly as she reached into her purse. "I like to see a boy take pride in his work. So many children just hurry through a job." Robert sighed with relief. She handed him a folded-up bill. Robert didn't bother unfolding it. He just knew it was the five dollars he needed.

He thanked her, raced home, and went straight to his room. He threw the money on his bed and went to get his piggy bank from the shelf. Then he stopped and looked back at his bed. The bill had partly uncurled when he threw it down and he could see the number one. It was only a one-dollar bill, not a five.

Robert sank down on his bed. He looked at his aching hands and fought off the urge to cry. For a minute he had almost liked Mrs. Sylvester. How dumb could he have been?

SIX

Two Squirrels and a Plum Tree

Mrs. Ott put some salve on Robert's blisters. "That's a lot of pain for a dollar," she said. "Maybe next time you should agree on a price before you start working."

"I'll never do any work for her again," Robert said.

Mrs. Ott put her arm around Robert's shoulders and gave him a sympathetic hug. "Honey, I don't think Mrs. Sylvester meant to cheat you. Sometimes old people get a little out of touch with what things cost. A dollar in her day was probably close to a whole day's wages. Besides, I think she has only a small income to live on. Maybe that's all she could afford. I'll tell you what. Why don't I give you the other four dollars you need?"

It was tempting, but Robert shook his head. "It wouldn't feel right," he said slowly. "I earned all the rest of the money, except for what I got on my birthday. I kind of wanted it to be something I earned myself."

Mrs. Ott looked surprised. "Goodness! You are growing up right before my very eyes. But you really did earn it. I'd just be giving it to you for Mrs. Sylvester."

"Thanks, Mom," Robert said. "But maybe I could do a job for you. Later, after my blisters heal." He grinned. "You pay better."

"That's a deal," Mrs. Ott said. "And you don't feel too angry toward Mrs. Sylvester?"

Robert shook his head. "I guess not. I never thought about her not having any money."

Friday night Aunt Frieda and Uncle John called all the way from Brazil. Harri was excited when she answered the call, but afterward she seemed sad and lost.

"The time will fly by until Christmas," Mrs. Ott told her gently. "You'll be too busy with school and making new friends to even notice. Your mother left some money to buy some new winter things. Tomorrow we'll go downtown and see what we can find. Would you like that?"

Harri sniffed a little, but she looked more cheerful.

"Would you like to come with us?" Mrs. Ott asked Robert.

Robert made a face and shook his head. He hated shopping.

The next morning, after Mrs. Ott and Harri left, Robert wandered down to the basement where his father was building a bookshelf. He loved to work with his father, measuring precisely and watching the electric saw cut perfectly straight lines. Mr. Ott said he had just the right personality for woodworking. Today, his father was staining the wood, rubbing it until it gleamed.

"Can I help?" Robert asked.

46

Mr. Ott looked at Robert's hands and shook his head. "I don't think you should risk getting the stain in those blisters. You can keep me company, though."

Robert stayed for a while, but it was boring just to watch. He decided it would be a good time to sit in his tree and finish reading his book.

Monster was tied up near the garage. He whined at Robert, his eyes sad. "She'll be back," Robert said. "Unfortunately." He stood just out of Monster's reach and watched the dog's tail make half circles in the dust as it wagged back and forth.

Robert carefully put out his hand, ready to pull it back the instant Monster lunged. But Monster looked friendly in spite of his giant size. Robert petted his silky black fur and Monster licked his hand.

"I'll bet your ancestors were sled dogs," Robert told him, sitting down and scratching the dog's ears. He imagined he was in the Arctic guiding a sled pulled by six dogs just like Monster. The snow was whipping across his face as he desperately sought some sign of civilization. "We have to get this medicine back to the settlement. People are counting on us. We—"

"I thought you were going to read your book," said Mr. Ott.

For a second Robert was surprised to see green grass and a blazing sun. "I just stopped to pet Monster," he said, feeling guilty.

Mr. Ott stroked Monster's head. "He's quite a dog, isn't he? He really adores Harri."

"How could anyone adore Harri?"

"Oh, come on now," Mr. Ott said cheerfully. "She isn't that bad. I really thought you two would learn to adjust. You are a lot alike in some ways."

Robert gave his father an incredulous look. Did he really believe that? The only thing they had in common was their dislike for each other. Aloud he said, "She just takes over everything. It's not the same with her here. Last night I even caught her lying on my bed reading a book. Her room is such a mess that she thinks she can take over mine."

Actually, he had found Harri lying in the half-dark, staring at the glow of Robert's well-dusted night-light, the book unopened.

Mr. Ott sighed. "I'll speak to her about that. But remember that she is a long way from home and we need to do all we can to make her comfortable here. And it certainly would help if you would quit sulking."

"I'm not sulking."

"What do you call it when someone goes around all day with his face all scrunched up, looking mad? It's depressing."

Robert didn't answer. After his father went back to his workshop he climbed up into the plum tree, intending to read. But his thoughts were full of Harri and Monster and he couldn't concentrate. He leaned his head against the trunk and closed his eyes.

"Just what is that book you've been laboring over all week?" Mrs. Sylvester was peering up at him.

Robert jumped. He hadn't heard her squeeze through the hedges. He reached down and handed her the book. "My teacher told me to read it."

Mrs. Sylvester flipped through the pages. "Pretty dry stuff. Have you ever read anything really good?"

Robert shrugged. "Mrs. Shoemaker had us read some other things. They were okay. I'd rather write my own stories, though."

"If you are going to be a writer, you have to read some good books," Mrs. Sylvester said firmly. "You come with me."

Robert swung down from the tree and reluctantly followed Mrs. Sylvester into her musty house. She marched straight to the ship room and stood thoughtfully in front of the bookshelf. "Ah. Here it is," she said, pulling out a book and handing it to him. She chuckled. "Don't look so miserable. This one you'll like, I promise."

Robert looked at the title: *The Lion, the Witch and the Wardrobe* by C. S. Lewis.

"There is a whole set of them called the Chronicles of Narnia. This is Book One. If you like it, you can read the others. They belonged to my husband. He taught school and his students always loved them. Now promise me you'll try it."

"I will," Robert promised doubtfully as Mrs. Sylvester led him to the door. He trudged back to the plum tree, opened the book, and read the first line.

When Mrs. Ott and Harri returned from their shopping trip, he was still reading. He put the book down only when Mrs. Ott called him to dinner. It was hard for him to believe that Mrs. Sylvester would know about a writer as wonderful as C. S. Lewis.

Harri squashed her peas in with her potatoes and

covered them with gravy. Robert tried not to look. "After we went shopping we stopped at a pet store," she told Mr. Ott. "I love animals, Fred. I think I might be a veterinarian when I grow up."

Mr. Ott raised his eyebrows when Harri used his first name, but said nothing. Robert guessed he was used to it by now.

"That's a nice ambition," Mrs. Ott said. "Robert likes animals, too."

Harri's look said plainly that she was not the least bit interested in what Robert liked. But Robert's mind was so filled with Mrs. Sylvester's book he didn't care. As soon as dinner was over he planned to climb back into the tree and finish it.

But when they were through, Mrs. Ott asked him to clear the table and help with the dishes. Harri escaped by saying she had to walk Monster. Robert pressed his lips together, but he knew it was useless to complain. He hurried through his chores and headed outside with his book, still angry.

Monster and Harri were back from their walk. Monster was napping under the plum tree and Harri was hanging upside down by her knees from a branch. Within him Robert felt a tidal wave of anger. Harri might have taken over his house and his mother, but she wasn't going to take away his private spot.

"That's my tree," he shouted. "That's my secret spot."

Harri looked at him upside down. "I thought we were going to have club meetings here. And anyway, how can a *tree* be a secret spot?" she asked mildly.

50

"It just is," Robert yelled. "Now get out of there. And I don't want to be in a stupid club with you, either."

Silently Harri swung up to a sitting position. She stared at him for a second before she jumped down. "I know what is wrong with you, Robbie," she said. "You have a bad case of sibling rivalry."

"My name is Robert," he responded, gritting his teeth. He wasn't sure what sibling rivalry was, and he certainly wasn't going to ask Harri. But she provided an explanation anyway. "You and I are both only children," she said seriously. "We're not used to sharing things. So we fight like brothers and sisters. It's perfectly natural. I read all about it in one of Frieda's books."

"I don't see you sharing anything. All you do is complain and brag."

"I'm company," Harri said. "And I don't complain half as much as you do."

Before he could think of a nasty answer Harri pointed to the edge of the woods. She put her finger on her lips for silence.

Red and Nutty were there, sitting up on their hind legs. Their tails twitched rapidly from side to side, as they watched with bright black eyes. With a pang Robert realized he'd forgotten to bring any bread.

"They are so cute," Harri whispered. "They don't even seem afraid of us."

"They're mine," Robert said proudly. For a moment he forgot his anger. "I've been feeding them every day all summer and now they will come right up to me." He could see by the look on Harri's face that she was impressed. "I named them Red and Nutty."

51

"Boring names," said Harri. "Why don't you name them something interesting?"

"Like what?" Robert said, getting angry again.

"Oh, I don't know. How about Artokulas for the larger one?"

"What's Artokulas mean?"

"Nothing. I just made it up," Harri said. "Come on, Artokulas," she coaxed Nutty.

Monster chose that moment to wake up from his sound sleep. He spied the squirrels and dashed after them, barking happily. After a startled second Red and Nutty dashed up a tree, scolding furiously. Monster circled the tree, still barking.

"Now look what your stupid dog did," Robert yelled. "They will probably never come back."

Harri looked stricken. "I'm sorry," she cried. "Monster didn't mean any harm. He just wants to play."

But Robert felt all the anger of the past few days come tumbling out of him. He tried not to see Harri's white face. He tried not to think about his parents' request that he make Harri feel at home. "Everything was fine before you and your stupid dog came," he said. "I wish you would just get out of my life." He turned around and marched back to the house, but halfway there he stopped. Harri was still standing in the same spot, a forlorn look on her face. "And stay away from my tree," he yelled.

SEVEN

Is Mr. Cross Cross?

It was the first day of school. In spite of Robert's pleading, his parents insisted that he walk to school with Harri.

"We are counting on you to help her get acquainted," Mr. Ott told him. "And to keep her company after school."

He waited impatiently by the door. He always left the house exactly at 8:30. That gave him just the right amount of time to walk to school and still have ten minutes to talk to Scott and Jason before the bell. Scott had been away the whole summer and Jason lived too far away to visit very often. He was especially anxious to catch up with them. But Harri was running late, mostly because she had changed her clothes four times before deciding what to wear.

"Why don't you lay out your clothes each night like I do?" he said impatiently.

"How would I know what I'm going to be in the mood to wear in the morning?" Harri asked.

It was almost 8:45 when they walked out the door. "We are going to be late because of you," Robert grumbled.

"Not if we run," Harri said. Without warning she broke into a sprint. By the time Robert recovered she was half a block ahead. She stopped and waited for him at the corner. He marched across the street without speaking. He might have to walk to school with her, but he had no intention of introducing her to his friends.

But when they reached the playground, Scott and Jason were leaning against the corner of the building, waiting for him. Scott grinned, and Jason whistled so loud that everyone on the playground turned around to look.

"Who's your girlfriend?" Scott asked, still grinning.

Robert knew his face was red. "She's not a friend. She's my cousin and she's staying with us."

A hurt look slipped across Harri's face, but he ignored her and pushed his way through the crowd of children reading the room assignments posted on the school door. He was holding a new folder and a box with new crayons, eraser, and pens, and he shifted them around in his arms so he could cross his fingers one last time. Mrs. Ott had registered Harri a few days before. If he was lucky she would be put in a different classroom. He could not be responsible for helping her make friends then. He even crossed his eyes for luck, but he had to uncross them to read the notice.

He examined Mrs. Clark's class assignments first. He remembered her from the year before. Robert had heard her yelling at her students clear downstairs in Mrs. Shoemaker's classroom. He was happy to see his name was not on her list. He looked at the other room assignment. There was his name, Scott's, and also Jason's. Clear down at the bottom, as though it had been added at the last minute, *Harriet Ann McDonald* was penciled in. Robert was so unhappy he almost didn't notice who the other teacher was: Mr. Cross. That was a surprise. Robert had never had a male teacher before. He hoped he wasn't like his name.

Harri was peering over his shoulder. "We're in the same room," she said. He couldn't tell from her voice if she was glad. He brushed past her and joined his friends at the door, leaving Harri standing by herself.

Some of the teachers were calling out names, gathering up the children assigned to them. Mr. Cross was not among them. The students in his room gathered together to talk.

"What is your cousin like?" Scott asked.

"A pest," Robert answered. "I can't wait until she leaves."

"How long is she going to stay?" Jason wanted to know.

"A whole year," Robert sighed.

"That's awful," both boys said at once, just as the bell rang.

Robert forgot about Harri as they trooped into the school. This year they were up with the big kids. Kindergarten through third grades were on the first floor, but fourth, fifth, and sixth grades were upstairs. They found Room 202, a bright, cheerful space with big windows, and searched for seats together in the middle of the room. If they sat in front the teacher would stare at them all day. The back was always watched carefully because the troublemakers usually tried to sit there.

"You will find your names on your desks," said a man standing at the front of the room. He was young and looked nervous. Robert hadn't even noticed him. "Since I am new," the teacher continued, "and don't know your names, I have put you in alphabetical order."

A subdued groan went up from all the children in the room. Robert figured in his head. Scott's last name was Adams. That meant he would be in the first seat, nowhere near Robert. Jason's last name was Bond. He would be close to Scott. Glumly, Robert looked for his seat. It was in the middle, close to where he was standing. Harri sat down in the seat right in front of him. *McDonald, Ott.* There were no *N*'s. Not only was Robert going to have to tolerate Harri at home, he would have to stare at her back all year.

Robert sat down and studied Mr. Cross. He wondered if it might be his first year as a teacher. He stood in front of the room and cleared his throat several times for attention. At last the students quieted down.

"Every year your teachers have probably asked you to write something about your summer," said Mr. Cross. "But the room looks a little bare to me, and I thought you could all draw your favorite summer memory while I pass out books. We can use the finished masterpieces to decorate the room. I've put out some

56

crayons and paper on the table in the back. Please take what you need quickly and return to your seats."

A girl named Mandy raised her hand.

"What do you mean, summer memory?" she asked.

"The nicest thing you did all summer," Mr. Cross explained. Everyone was soon busy except for Robert. He carefully arranged his new pencils and tablets in his desk while he tried to decide what to draw. The beach where they had taken their vacation early in the summer had been fun. Robert thought about the waves lapping at the shore and the walks they had taken, gathering seashells. They had stayed a whole week, but already Robert had trouble remembering exactly how it had looked. He glanced over at the boy next to him who was drawing a beach scene. The roller coaster at Pirate's Point was a good summer memory. Robert remembered the thrill as the car hurtled down and he wasn't afraid. He had to hurry and make up his mind.

Mr. Cross was calling the students up to his desk in alphabetical order. "Your reading books will be based on your level last year," he told the class "but I'll be testing you sometime later this week. I hope you all improved over the summer."

Robert thought of the textbook he had left unfinished. But he had already asked Mrs. Sylvester for *Prince Caspian,* the second book in the Chronicles of Narnia. She had looked very pleased when he told her how much he loved *The Lion, the Witch and the Wardrobe.*

Mr. Cross was already to the *L*'s. Robert stared at the empty sheet of paper in front of him. If only he were sitting in his plum tree. He could think better there. Then it came to him. The nicest memory of the summer was the hours he'd spent in his tree.

"Robert Ott," called Mr. Cross. Robert jumped up, feeling guilty. He hadn't even started his picture. He went to the teacher's desk and stood quietly while Mr. Cross wrote down the numbers that were stamped on each of his books. The reading book was brand-new. Robert could tell by the fresh, never-used smell. It looked interesting until he peeked at Harri's book on his way back to his seat. Then he flushed with shame. It was not one but two levels above his. Now she would have something else to feel superior about. Harri looked up from her drawing and smiled, but Robert walked by and pretended not to see. He sank back down in his seat. Harri got up and went to the back of the room for more crayons. While she was gone Robert peered at her half-finished picture.

Harri had drawn herself driving across the country. Part of the picture was a desert with brown and red sand and cactus plants. Then there were the outlines of mountains, and on the other side, farm lands. It was a wonderful picture, the kind that was always hung in the halls for all the parents to see. Robert knew his drawing would not be nearly as good. He could see what he wanted to do in his head, but when he tried to put what was in his head on the paper, it always looked wrong. He colored a crude tree and made a stick boy beside it. Then he looked at the clock and forgot all about Harri. It was almost time for recess and the race.

EIGHT

The Race

Before the recess bell's last echo had died Robert and his friends had reached the playground.

"Are you ready?" Scott yelled.

Robert nodded and grinned. One of the nicest things about Elmwood Elementary was the playground. It was long and narrow, just right for running races. Almost every day Robert, Scott, and Jason ran races from the school building to the fence and back again. They had been doing it since kindergarten, and although Robert almost always won, Jason and Scott never stopped trying to beat him. Sometimes one of the bigger boys would join the race, but Robert could beat most of them, too. Robert loved to run. He loved the feel of air whooshing past his face and the way his ears played funny tricks and turned all the shouts and laughter into one big roar.

Scott had grown over the summer. Last year the

59

boys had been almost the same height. This year Scott was at least three inches taller than Robert.

"I'll bet I can beat you now," he teased Robert. "Mom had to buy me all new pants for school. My legs grew. That means I can take longer steps."

Robert grinned back at his friend. In a way it would be fun if Scott did win. It would make it more challenging.

It seemed as if everyone in the school had lined up to watch the first race of the year. Even the principal, Mr. Hadley, was watching from the steps. Scott, Robert, and Jason lined up against the wall.

One of their classmates offered to start the race. "On your mark, get set, GO," he shouted. Robert forgot everything except the pure joy of running. He hardly heard the shouts of the other children urging them on. They ran past a group of girls, and Harri's face was just a blur as Robert whizzed by. Scott was right beside him when they reached the fence. Robert put on an extra burst of speed and touched the fence an instant before Scott.

"Back again," everyone was shouting. Robert glanced at Scott to see if he had heard. But Scott was already heading back to the school wall. Robert pumped his legs as fast as they would go. He felt his heart hammering, but he knew he was the fastest runner in the world. He wondered if his legs looked like a blur to everyone who was watching. His feet pounded past Scott, and when they reached the building he was several strides ahead. Jason trailed far behind. Robert leaned against the building, gasping for breath.

Everyone was cheering. "No one is faster than Robert," one of the fifth-grade boys told another. Robert felt wonderful.

"You almost beat me," he said to Scott. "It was a good race."

"I just need some practice," Scott said. "I'll beat you tomorrow."

Robert was surprised to notice Harri among the group cheering. She was standing with Mandy and another classmate, Jennifer, talking excitedly.

"Harri's probably telling them about the track team at her school," Robert said to Jason. "But I'll bet she's never seen anyone as fast as us."

"Faster than a speeding bullet," Jason yelled, just as the bell rang. Laughing, the boys entered the school.

To Robert's surprise, Harri didn't wait for him after school. As he walked to the corner with Jason and Scott, he saw her ahead of them walking with Mandy. He had to walk the rest of the way alone because his friends went in the opposite direction. By the time he got home, Harri was already telling Mrs. Ott about Mr. Cross.

"He said my picture was wonderful and he put it on the door where everyone could see it. And he said when we study Texas he wants me to give a talk."

"That's wonderful," Mrs. Ott said warmly. "How about you, Robert? Did you have a good day?"

He shrugged. "It was okay. Mr. Cross gave us homework already." Then he looked at his mother in surprise. "Why are you home already?"

"I left early so I could be here on your first day back

61

at school. Hurry and change your clothes. I've got something to show you both."

It was nice having his mother home, but Robert suspected that she had done it just for Harri. He changed and took his school clothes to the hamper in the bathroom. By the time he returned to the kitchen, Harri was already waiting. The two of them followed Mrs. Ott to the yard.

"Just a quick peek," Mrs. Ott said, pointing to the birdhouse. "We don't want to disturb the mother."

"Babies," Harri squealed with delight.

"Four of them," Robert said, counting quickly.

"It's a good thing human babies don't do that," Harri laughed. She put her head back and opened her mouth like the tiny birds. "How would you like it if kids just sat around with their mouths open, waiting for food?"

Mrs. Ott chuckled, "Sometimes I think they do. And speaking of that, I suppose you two would like a snack?"

For an answer both Harri and Robert followed her into the house with their mouths wide open, tweeting like baby birds.

The next morning Harri was only a few minutes late, and Robert almost let himself believe things would get better. Maybe his parents were right and they just needed time to adjust.

But when they lined up for the race at recess, Harri was there. "Can I race with you?" she asked.

"No," said Robert. "This is our race."

"I don't care," Scott said. He whispered, "You know we'll beat her."

"Well, I don't want to race with her. It will just spoil everything." He glared at Harri.

"What's the matter? Afraid I'll beat you?" Harri jutted her chin out and stood her ground.

"Come on, let her try," several onlookers shouted.

Robert glared at her again. "All the way to the fence, and back."

A second later they were off, running like the wind, heading for the fence. Out of the corner of his eye Robert saw Harri, running beside Scott, right behind him. He was surprised, but not worried. It was a long way to the fence and back. She would not be able to keep up. He had to admit she was pretty fast. Poor Scott, he thought. He was going to be awfully embarrassed if he was beaten by a girl. He reached the fence and touched it as he made the turn.

Robert heard footsteps coming up behind him. He concentrated every bit of his mind on the wall ahead. But the footsteps were gaining and then someone was beside him. He turned his head slightly, hoping to see Jason or Scott. It wouldn't be too bad to lose to them. But it was Harri, racing ahead, touching the wall an instant before he did. He rested against the wall, panting, fighting to hold back the tears of frustration and shame.

"That was a great race," Harri said. "I love to run, don't you?"

Robert knew he should be a good sport. He knew he should tell Harri what a great race she had run. He knew just what to say. "Hey, Harri, you were really good.

Want to race tomorrow?" But while he was thinking those words, something very different came out of his mouth. "Why don't you go back home and leave me alone?" he shouted. Then he pushed past the group of fourth graders gathered at the door and stomped into the school.

NINE

The Worst Day

"She was just lucky," Scott said at lunch.

"I'll bet she couldn't do it again," Jason said. "Why don't you race with her tomorrow?"

Robert glared at Harri, who was sitting two tables away with Jennifer, Mandy, and several other girls from their class. Winning the race had instantly made her popular. The girls were giggling and every once in a while one of them would look over at his table. Robert felt his ears get red. They were laughing at him, he just knew it.

He thought about Jason's suggestion all afternoon. If he challenged Harri to another race, she might win again. It was a hard decision to make.

Robert walked home slowly after school, hoping that by the time he got there Harri and Monster would be out for a walk. He would take *Prince Caspian* and sit in his tree until his mother called him for dinner. After dinner he'd try writing in his journal. Sometimes that helped him make up his mind.

Sally Anne rode by on her bike. Today she had gold fingernails and her hair frizzed like cotton candy around her face.

"Hi," she said, rolling to a stop. "Need anything at the corner grocery?"

Robert just shook his head.

"How is school this year?" she asked.

"I have a man teacher," Robert said glumly. "He gave us three pages of vocabulary words to look up."

"In one night?"

"He gave us three weeks," Robert admitted.

"Wait until you get to high school," Sally Anne said. "Then you'll have to do it all in one night. I've got a ton of homework already. That's why I'm going to the store. I can't think without gum. And anyway," she said with a grin, "Jeffrey got a job there after school."

When Robert arrived home he was surprised to find Monster on the front porch. He opened the door and the dog wiggled and jumped, covering him with slobbery kisses. Robert scratched Monster's ears. The house didn't seem so empty and quiet with Monster there to greet him. He wondered where Harri was. It wasn't like her to leave Monster behind.

He heard voices when he walked out to the backyard a few minutes later. He stood staring, unable to believe his eyes. The plum tree was filled with girls.

Harri poked her head out from between the branches. "This is a meeting of the F.G.O. Club," she

67

called out. "That means For Girls Only. So stay out, Robbie."

"That's my tree," Robert gasped. "And don't call me that."

Harri shrugged. "I asked Margaret if we could have a club here and she said yes."

Robert was speechless. He turned and headed back to the house, but the sound of their laughter followed his every step.

"He must still be mad because you won the race," he heard Mandy say.

"Don't pay any attention to him," Harri's taunting voice answered. "He's just a spoiled baby. He's even afraid to sleep without a light."

More laughter echoed from the tree, but Robert jerked open the door and flung himself inside. His journal was on the kitchen table. In a rage he flipped it open to the first empty page, and in big ugly letters he wrote *I hate Harri.*

The girls were leaving. He could hear them through the open kitchen window, still laughing, saying their good-byes. Then Mrs. Ott's car pulled into the driveway. The car door slammed and he heard her say a warm "hello" to Harri. Robert grabbed his journal and headed for his room, still too angry to talk.

Harri's door was open. He hesitated, wishing he could think of some way to get even. Her room was a mess, as usual. Something caught his eye, poking out from under the bed. It was the stuffed monkey, the one Harri had tried to hide the day he'd watched her unpack. He crossed the room quickly and picked it up.

Most of the fur had worn off and the tail was matted as though it had been chewed. And she called me a baby, he thought. He wondered what Harri's new friends would think if they knew she still took a stuffed monkey to bed.

Mrs. Ott and Harri were walking into the house, chatting comfortably. Robert stuffed the monkey back into its hiding place and went to the kitchen.

"You should have seen Robert's face when I won," Harri was saying when he entered the room.

Mrs. Ott gave Robert an understanding look, but he turned away. Harri didn't seem to notice. "All the girls started talking to me and now we're going to have a club. They came over this afternoon to make plans, but we thought we'd meet on Saturdays if that's all right."

"Of course it is, dear," Mrs. Ott said. "I'm glad you're making friends."

"Why did you tell Harri she could have her friends in my tree?" Robert demanded, his anger pouring out.

Mrs. Ott looked startled. "I didn't."

"You said I could have friends over, and that I was part of the family." Harri's voice was rising. "How can I be part of the family if I'm not even allowed in a dumb old plum tree?"

Mrs. Ott looked tired. "Are you in the club, Robert?"

"I asked him," Harri said. "But he wouldn't join. So this club is just for girls."

"The tree is Robert's special place," Mrs. Ott said after a moment. "But perhaps he would share it just with you. Why don't you have your club meet in the

69

house? It might not be safe to have so many children in the tree, anyway."

"That sounds like a good solution to me," said Mr. Ott. He had arrived home in the middle of the disagreement. Harri looked surprised when Robert nodded without further argument, but she nodded, too.

Robert was still angry, but he tried to hide it for the rest of the evening. He even managed to ask Harri politely to return the dictionary to its proper place on the bookshelf so he could work on his vocabulary. But in the morning, after Harri had left her room, he snuck in and found the toy monkey, which he stuffed into a sack.

Robert waited until recess for his revenge. Scott and Jason looked curiously at the sack he carried, but Robert said nothing until the entire class had reached the playground.

"You know, I've been thinking, Harri," he said. "Maybe we could race this morning after all."

"Great." Harri smiled at him in surprise.

"And you had better carry your little night-night monkey for luck," he said loudly, whipping it out of the sack.

A bright red flush crept over Harri's face. "Give me that," she shouted. Laughing, Robert threw it to one of the fifth-grade boys standing nearby. He thought the boy would throw it back, but instead he tossed it to another boy. Back and forth the monkey was flung around the playground, and all the while Harri was running, trying to catch it. Angry tears filled her eyes, and Robert saw a bit of stuffing come loose and fall to the ground.

Suddenly, it was no longer funny. Robert had a sick feeling in his stomach as the monkey was tossed from child to child. It was coming apart right before his eyes. First a leg fell off, and then the tail. Harri scrambled after each piece, sobbing silently.

"Give it back," he shouted. Finally the bigger boys tired of the cruel game and tossed the mangled monkey to Robert. He handed it to a tearful Harri. "I'm sorry," he mumbled. "I didn't mean for this to happen. I was just mad because of yesterday."

"I've had this since I was a baby," Harri said, hugging the tattered remains. "Now it's ruined."

"I just wanted you to see what it was like to be laughed at," Robert said. "But I'm sorry it got torn."

"I think you are the meanest and most selfish person I ever met." Harri wiped a hand across her eyes and walked away.

"It was just a dumb old stuffed monkey," Jason said loyally. Robert shrugged, but in his heart he was afraid that Harri was right.

TEN

Reading and Writing and Races

Mr. Cross handed out notebooks as soon as school started the next morning. "I want everyone to do a little writing for me this year. You are to write every day. It doesn't have to be a long piece, but I do want it to tell something about you. You can write stories that tell how you feel about something, or even a poem. The important part is to keep at it."

Most of the class groaned, but Robert felt the thickness of the notebook with delight.

"You are also to read two books every month," Mr. Cross went on. "When you get done with each one I want you to write a book report telling me about the book and how you liked it."

"How big a book do we have to read?" Scott asked.

"As big as you can, but it should be at least fifty pages," answered Mr. Cross.

Most of the class groaned again, but Robert smiled

secretly. He was halfway finished with *Prince Caspian*. There were six books in the Narnia Chronicles—three months' worth of reports. And Mrs. Sylvester could probably suggest other titles he could ask for at the library.

Harri had ignored him throughout the previous evening and she hadn't mentioned the incident of the monkey to his parents. Robert wondered if she would still want to race. When the recess bell ran he brushed past her and ran outside.

The boys stood up against the wall. Scott and Jason looked at Robert. "What are we going to do?" Scott whispered. "Here she comes."

Harri and Mandy walked up to the wall. "Are we going to race today?" Harri asked.

"They're too scared a girl will beat them again," said Mandy.

"We're not," said Robert. There was no way out of it. If he didn't race, it would be all over school that he was afraid of a girl. He would beat her this time, he told himself. He just had to.

"They're going to race again," said one of the fifth graders. Everyone was crowding to the end of the playground to watch. "Just Robert and Harri this time," someone suggested.

Someone yelled, "Ready, set, GO." Robert leaped ahead. For a second he forgot about Harri. He forgot about everything except the joy of running fast, the sting of the wind against his face. He felt that any moment his feet would leave the ground and he would fly.

At the fence Robert was slightly ahead. He knew Harri was almost beside him. Any second now she would put on her sudden burst of speed. He concentrated on the building straight ahead. He had to win, he just had to. He turned his head and saw that she was only a step behind. But then he was at the wall. He reached out his hand and touched it. He had won!

"I knew you could do it," Scott yelled, pounding him on the back.

The girls in their class looked disappointed. "You are really fast," Harri said, leaning against the building and panting. "I guess I was just lucky the other day."

"You run pretty good, for a girl," Jason said generously.

People crowded around, congratulating Robert. He looked at Harri and saw a strange look in her eyes. There was a funny feeling in the back of Robert's mind, but he didn't let himself think about it.

Sally Anne was sitting on her front porch when Robert walked by on his way home from school. High school started earlier in the morning, and so she was often home before Robert. "Hi." She waved listlessly.

"What's the matter?" he asked.

"Jeffrey and I broke up," she said.

"That's too bad," said Robert, although he suspected that Sally Anne's romance with Jeffrey was mostly wishful thinking.

She gave Robert a thoughtful look. "You're a boy. Would you ask me for a date if you were older?"

Robert squirmed uncomfortably. "Maybe. If you

didn't wear purple nail polish."

He left Sally Anne looking at her nails in a thoughtful way, and hurried home. He went straight to his room, and by the time his mother peeked in to say hello, he was totally absorbed in his book. He waved at her and went back to reading. Later he heard the buzz of the gasoline-powered weed cutter in the woods, which meant his father was home, too.

Robert picked his way through a jungle of weeds and berry bushes that had grown up under the trees, making it difficult to walk. Mr. Ott was cutting a trail through them.

"Hi," he said when he saw Robert. He turned off the motor and sat on a stump to rest. "I've been meaning to do this all summer."

Robert looked down at his father's head.

"You've got a bald spot," he exclaimed.

Mr. Ott reached up and touched the spot with his fingers. "Great," he said with a rueful look. "Just what I wanted to hear."

"It's not very bad," Robert said. "Do you think I will be bald someday?"

Mr. Ott smiled. "Maybe. But I wouldn't worry about it. It's not something you can change."

Robert sighed. "It doesn't seem fair. Some things that shouldn't change, do, and then when you want to change something, you can't."

"It would be an awfully boring life if nothing changed," said Mr. Ott. "Everything does, you know. Even the Earth. Some changes are so slow we don't even notice them. Others take some getting used to. But in the end, change makes life more interesting."

"Not Harri," Robert said. "There is nothing interesting about her."

"Oh, so that's what we're talking about," Mr. Ott said, nodding. "Well, as I see it you have three choices."

"Three?"

"Yup. You can sulk and stew until June, which might be hard to do. You can try to pretend she isn't here, which also might be hard to do. Or you can make friends with her. That might be hard to do, too, but not as hard as the other two."

"That's what you think," Robert said.

Mr. Ott stood and picked up the weed cutter. "Well, I can't make you like her. But if you can work out your problems with Harri, you two might have a very special friendship. Harri could learn a lot from you, Robert," Mr. Ott said seriously. "And maybe you could learn some things from her."

Robert thought about his father's words as he walked back to the house. Maybe he should try harder to be friends. But when he came out of the woods, Harri was sitting high in the plum tree, picking plums just like she owned them. Seeing her in the tree made Robert forget all his good intentions of a minute earlier. This was war. A plum tree war. He crept up quietly and then, when he was right beside the tree, he shouted as loudly as he could, "GET OUT OF MY TREE!"

To Robert's surprise, Harri jumped down from the tree without a word and headed for the house. Robert thought she looked sad. For a second Robert felt sorry. But then he shook his head. It served her right. She could find her own special place—maybe somewhere in China.

ELEVEN

Spiders and Santa Claus

"What are you going to be?" Scott asked.

Robert shrugged. It was almost time for Elmwood's yearly Halloween parade. On the last school day before Halloween, parents were invited to watch the kids from each classroom march around the playground and show off their costumes. Prizes were given for the best ones. In kindergarten Robert had won first prize for the cutest costume. He had been dressed up in a bunny suit. It was embarrassing even to think about it now. This year he wanted to win for being the scariest. The last two years he had tried to win as Count Dracula. The trouble was, there were always a lot of Count Draculas. He needed to do something really different, but so far he hadn't come up with any ideas.

"I wanted to be Dracula," Jason said. "But my mom says we can't afford a new costume and she hasn't got time to make one. So I guess I'll have to be Superman again."

"You can use my costume from last year," Robert said. "It's too little for me. All you would have to do is buy some fangs."

"That would be great," said Jason. He practiced his vampire voice. "I vant to drink your blood."

It was noon recess and the boys were sitting on the monkey bars. They hardly ever raced anymore. Somehow it wasn't as much fun. Harri walked by with Mandy on the way to the swings. "I got a letter from my parents yesterday," Harri was saying. "They are coming home for Christmas, for two weeks. We'll spend it in Dallas, of course. Frieda says she wants to be somewhere warm."

"Wow." Mandy sounded impressed. "I'll bet you'll be glad to see your friends."

The letter had come for Harri the day before. Robert had wanted to look at the interesting stamps, but Harri had taken the envelope into her room. A few minutes later she had come out screeching with excitement. For the rest of the evening Harri had talked about the Christmas trip. Robert hadn't really minded. Two weeks without Harri in the house, he'd thought gleefully.

Jason jumped down from the monkey bars and started to chase Harri and Mandy, his hands scrunched up like claws. "Just one little bite," he yelled. "Then you will be in my power forever."

The girls screamed in mock terror and ran away. Jason chased them for a few minutes before he returned, panting and grinning from ear to ear. Robert was disgusted. Why was Jason acting that way with

79

Harri, of all people? It almost looked as if Jason liked her.

Harri walked back to the monkey bars. "What are you going to be for Halloween?" she asked Scott.

Robert turned away. They hardly ever argued anymore. At home they mostly ignored each other and at school they stayed with their own friends. Harri's F.G.O. Club met every Saturday in Harri's room. Mostly the meetings consisted of the girls fixing their hair and talking about boys.

"I think I am going to be a knight. My brother has this terrific sword. It's really made out of plastic, but it looks real," Scott answered.

"I'm going to be Santa Claus," Harri said, even though no one had asked. "Fred said I could wear an old Santa Claus suit he has."

"You can't be Santa Claus for Halloween," Robert said.

"Why not? I'll carry a sack over my back, but instead of toys it will be filled with candy."

"I think that's a great idea," said Jason, whose love of candy was well known. "I'll bet no one has ever thought of that before."

"I'm going to ask Margaret to help me take it in so it fits. Then I'm going to tie some branches on Monster so he can be a reindeer."

"That will be neat," said Jason. "As long as Dracula doesn't get him. I vant to drink Santa's blood," he shouted. Laughing, Harri darted away again with Jason in close pursuit.

Robert sighed. He knew Harri had a terrific idea. She was sure to win the prize for the most original costume.

Mr. Cross gave the class a practice spelling test after lunch. Every Wednesday there was a practice test. Students who missed one word or less didn't have to take the test on Friday. Every week Robert passed the Wednesday test. Harri always had to take it over on Friday. Mr. Cross had moved Robert up one level in reading. And he had told Robert that he was doing such wonderful book reports that by Christmas he could expect to move up to Harri's group. They were reading at the fifth-grade level.

Today Robert's mind was on costumes and he couldn't concentrate on the spelling words. Twice he had to ask Mr. Cross to repeat a word.

"*Spider,*" said Mr. Cross. "Where is your mind today, Robert? I think you must have Halloween fever."

Robert bent over his paper and spelled out s-p-i-d-e-r. That was easy. In his mind he pictured a hairy black spider. Then suddenly he sat up straight in his chair. That was it. He would be a tarantula for Halloween. His mom would help him make a suit of creepy black fur. Robert had seen a tarantula in a pet store once. The man at the counter had assured him that they made good pets. But Robert could remember how horrible it looked. If he could win a prize for the scariest costume, he wouldn't feel so bad if Harri won a prize, too.

"*Veranda,*" said Mr. Cross. Robert hurried to write it down. He had a feeling he had missed a word while he was thinking. He would probably have to take the test again on Friday. But he was so happy with his idea that he didn't even care.

Mrs. Ott looked upset when he explained his idea that evening. "I'm not sure I'm that creative. And Harri has already asked me to take in the Santa suit. I don't know if I will have time."

"Harri is going to have a prize-winning costume and I won't have anything," he pleaded.

"I didn't say that. Of course you'll have something. How about a ghost? I've got some old sheets we could use."

"Can't you just think how terrific a spider would be? All we need is really awful hairy cloth."

"Wait a minute," Mrs. Ott exclaimed. "I did see a remnant of some fuzzy material last time I was shopping. I guess we could dye it black. It might be fun to see what we can do." She looked at him. "Did you notice I said 'we'?"

Robert nodded happily. His mother bought the material the very next day, and each afternoon Robert cut out spider legs while his mother sewed. His arms and legs would fit into four of the legs. The other four legs they stuffed. Robert didn't tell anyone about his costume. He and his mother worked in her bedroom, so not even Harri had seen it.

At last, with only two days to go until the Halloween parade, the costume was finished. Robert slipped it on while his mother made the last few adjustments. It was wonderful. The material felt like silky fur, and dyed black it looked just like a real hairy spider. His mother sewed two large red glass buttons on the hood so that they hung down over his forehead. When he hunched over to walk he really did look like a giant red-eyed spider slinking across the room. He just knew he was going to win first prize for the scariest costume.

"It's wonderful," Robert said.

"It had better be, after all that work." Mrs. Ott sighed. "And don't grow, so you can wear it next year."

Robert went to the living room to show Mr. Ott. Monster was sleeping by the fireplace. Now that the Otts had become fond of the dog, he was sometimes allowed in the house. But when Monster saw the giant spider he jumped up and growled.

"Monster thinks it's real." Mr. Ott chuckled.

"It is neat," said Harri, looking up from her book. "I'll bet you win the prize for the scariest costume." She had been in a good mood ever since she received her parents' letter, and she sounded almost friendly.

"You have some room on the shelf in your closet, Harri," said Mrs. Ott. "I'll put the costumes there until the parade on Friday."

Robert reluctantly took off the costume and gave it to his mother to put away. It would be hard to wait two more days. He was going to win the prize. He just knew it.

TWELVE

Monsters and Spiders?

Friday was cool but the sun was shining. It was a perfect day for the Halloween parade. Robert smiled, thinking of earlier years when his costume had been spoiled by having to wear a heavy coat. Mr. Cross had promised they could put on the costumes right after lunch. Parents were invited at two, and Mrs. Ott was going to come home at noon and bring their costumes and Monster to school.

"Ho, ho, ho," said Harri in a loud voice as she walked into the kitchen for breakfast. She had modeled her costume for the Otts the night before. Her long braids had been tucked up in a red stocking cap and she had worn a fake beard. She had even rubbed some of Mrs. Ott's lipstick on her nose to make it look red, and she was holding a very unhappy Monster by a rope. Monster had been dressed in a red sweater, and a pair of cardboard antlers was tied on his head. It was a great costume, Robert thought. But not as good as his.

"It's wonderful. I hope you both win," Mrs. Ott had said.

Robert waited impatiently for Harri to finish dressing. They still left together every morning, because his parents had made him responsible for locking up the house, but Harri met Mandy and Jennifer on the corner and walked with them.

"See you at lunchtime," Mrs. Ott said, giving him a peck on the cheek. "Don't forget to shut Monster on the porch."

"Hurry up," Robert yelled after his mother left. "I don't want to be late."

Harri raced into the kitchen, her eyes sparkling with excitement. "Have you seen Monster's red sweater?" she gasped.

Robert glared at her. "Isn't it with the rest of your costume?"

Harri looked around distractedly. "Maybe I threw it back in the closet." She ran back into her room, Monster at her heels.

"For Pete's sake, *hurry,*" Robert yelled again. He checked the porch to make sure that Monster had food and water for the day and sat at the table to wait. Harri's room was silent. "Come on," he shouted.

The silence from Harri's room was shattered by a low scream and strange thumping sounds he couldn't identify. Monster was growling, and the thumping sounds grew louder. Robert jumped out of the chair and ran to Harri's door.

"What's the matter?" he yelled. There was no response. And a second later he yelled again. "What are

85

you doing?" He hesitated a moment, then slowly opened the door.

Robert stood stock still in the doorway. Harri was standing by the open closet door, white-faced, and the spider suit was ripped apart, tossed about the room. Little bits of stuffing still floated through the air before coming to land on the dressers, bed, and rug.

He couldn't even yell. He just stood there, looking at what was left of his costume, and fought back angry tears.

"Bad dog," he finally screamed. Monster slid under the bed to hide. Harri looked at Robert miserably.

"Don't yell at Monster," she said in a shaky voice. "It was my fault. I pulled your costume out of my closet looking for Monster's sweater. He grabbed it so fast. . . ."

Robert bent down and scooped up handfuls of stuffing. "You did this on purpose," he said softly. "Because of the monkey."

"It was an accident," Harri insisted. "It really was. Please don't be mad. You can wear my Santa suit, if you want." A single tear rolled down her cheek.

"I don't want your stupid Santa suit." Robert was screaming. "I hate you. I hate everything about you. Everything was fine until you came. You don't belong here anyway. Just take your stupid costume and get out of here. And don't ever come back." Robert ran to his room and slammed the door.

Robert could hear Harri moving around in her room. He was going to be late for school, but he didn't care. He didn't care if he ever went to school again.

86

After a while the house was quiet. Robert wondered if Harri had gone to school. He thought about Harri winning a prize and all the parents clapping and cheering. Finally he got up and went to her room.

The spider costume was lying on her bed. Harri had picked up the loose filling and stuffed it back inside. It wasn't as bad as he had first thought. Two of the legs were loose, but maybe his mother would have time to repair them when she came home. Then he saw the Santa suit. It was on the table and there was a note next to it.

> I am running away. Please keep Monster and
> give him a good home. I know you like him
> and I don't have any way to take care of him.
> I'm really, really sorry about the spider suit.
> Don't try to find me because I will be far
> away. (Maybe in Africa.)
>   Harri

She's bluffing, Robert thought. She wouldn't really run away. He looked in the dresser drawers and closet. They were nearly empty and the big suitcase was missing, too. He sat on the bed to think.

Robert looked at the clock. School would be starting in fifteen minutes. Mr. Cross would take attendance, and then the school would call Mrs. Sylvester to find out what had happened to them. There was a chance he could find Harri before that. She couldn't go very fast carrying the heavy suitcase. But which way did she go? In a movie he'd seen once, police detectives checked the bus station and the airport, looking for a missing person. But Mount Stanton didn't have an airport or a bus station. What if Harri asked someone for a ride, and she was kidnapped!

Robert ran out to the road and scanned both directions. Harri was nowhere in sight. He considered telling Mrs. Sylvester and asking her to call the police. But what if they got mad and locked Harri in jail? It was probably against the law to run away. Robert knew he could call his mother, but Harri would really be in trouble then.

Then Robert remembered Monster. Harri loved Monster more than anything and Monster loved Harri. He could find her.

Robert looked under Harri's bed. Monster was still there. His brown eyes looked hopeful and his tail thumped softly on the rug. Robert coaxed him out. "I'm sorry I yelled at you," Robert said, patting the dog's head. "You've got to find Harri. Do you understand? Find Harri."

Monster's tail thumped on the rug. He followed Robert outside and sniffed at the grass as though he really understood. Then he charged away, headed, not for the street, but for the woods behind the house. "Oh, no," Robert groaned as he saw a streak of red fur at the edge of the woods. He should have tied Monster with a leash. Because Monster wasn't looking for Harri. He was chasing Red and Nutty.

"Come back, you stupid dog," Robert called. But Monster kept running until he disappeared into the woods.

THIRTEEN

The Accident

Robert plunged into the woods after Monster. He stopped every few minutes to call or whistle. He could follow Monster by the sound of barking ahead of him as he ran. He was grateful for his father's newly made path. At least he wouldn't have to add poison ivy to his list of problems.

"Come back, you stupid dog," he yelled in frustration. In the summer the woods were a noisy buzz of insects and chirping birds. Now, suddenly, they were quiet. A hush settled over the trees as if the forest were holding its breath, waiting to see what would happen next.

Then Robert thought he heard a sound. He listened carefully and heard it again—a soft whining sound like Monster made when he was excited. Robert left the path and crashed through the woods.

He found Harri's suitcase in a clearing near a large rock. Monster had found her after all. He could just glimpse Monster plunging through the woods, and ahead of the dog the yellow flash of Harri's sweater. He raced after them. Monster was acting as if this was a new kind of game. He barked excitedly as he ran, making it easy for Robert to follow.

Brown leaves crunched under Robert's feet. The frost had come only a few days before and the trees still had half their foliage. Harri's sweater blended perfectly with the red and gold leaves. Several times he lost sight of her and had to stop and listen. Too bad that Harri is such a fast runner, he thought. But of course, he could run faster than she could. He had proved that in the second race, hadn't he? As he ran Robert let thoughts come that he had pushed away that day at school. Harri had let him win. He stopped for an instant. Why would she do that? Robert ran on again, knowing the answer. She had let him win because she had really wanted to be friends.

"Harri, wait," he yelled. "I've got to talk to you."

He caught sight of Harri again. She had almost reached the road. The woods thinned here, and Robert saw her hesitate and look back, as though she had heard him.

At the same instant there was a terrible crash in the bushes at the edge of the woods. A female deer ran straight into the road. Robert, still moving at top speed, heard a motor, and at almost the same second the squeal of brakes and an awful thud.

Harri's eyes were wide with shock. Robert knew it was their wild race through the woods that had startled the doe. He didn't want to look, but he made himself

91

walk beyond the trees. Harri was there. She reached out and held his hand, and together they stepped to the edge of the road, dreading what they would see. Monster was sniffing around the bushes where the doe had been.

A blue car had pulled over to the side of the road, its fender badly dented. A bald man with a rumpled business suit was bending over the still body of the doe. When he saw them, he stood up straight.

"It jumped right out in front of me."

Robert nodded, swallowing the lump in his throat. "Is it dead?"

" 'Fraid so," said the man. "Say, shouldn't you kids be in school?"

"We had kind of a family emergency," Robert told him. Harri gave him a strange look. He smiled at her weakly and squeezed her hand.

"Well, I'm kind of in a hurry," the man said. "Do you suppose you two could call the sheriff and report this for me? They have people to take care of these things."

The man had been moving back to his car as he spoke. He climbed in and slammed the door. "Don't look so upset. It's just a deer. Happens all the time." He drove off in a hurry.

"He should have waited," Robert said, looking at the deer.

"I guess we had better go tell somebody," Harri said. "Come on, Monster."

Monster was still hunkered down by the bushes. He whined softly, but didn't come to Harri's call.

92

"Come on," Harri called impatiently, but Robert had spotted something in the shadows under the brush, and he motioned for Harri to be quiet.

"Monster's found something," he said softly.

Monster stood up as they came closer. He wagged his tail but otherwise didn't move.

"It's a fawn," Harri exclaimed in a choked voice.

The fawn, very young for that time of year, was crouched back, nearly hidden in the brown leaves. Its huge eyes looked frightened, and it staggered to its feet as if it might run. But Robert put his arms around the fawn and together he and Harri talked softly until it stopped trembling.

"I think it's a little female," said Robert.

"What should we do?" Harri asked.

"It's our fault the mother got killed. We have to take her home and take care of her."

"How will we get her home?" Harri said doubtfully. "She's not very old, but she's still too big for us to carry."

Monster edged closer to the tiny deer, and the fawn reached out delicately until its nose touched the dog's.

"Go home, Monster," Harri shouted. With a hurt look, Monster backed away.

"No, wait," said Robert. "The fawn doesn't seem afraid of Monster at all. I have an idea." He ran back to the road where the doe lay. She appeared almost to be sleeping. Only a small trickle of blood told the true story. Swallowing his tears, Robert ran his hands over the doe's body. Then he ran back to Monster and rubbed his hands on the dog.

"Maybe the fawn will follow Monster if he smells like her mother," he said.

They held their breaths, waiting for the fawn's reaction.

The trick seemed to work. After an anxious moment the fawn walked toward the dog.

"That was a fantastic idea," said Harri. "You are really clever."

Robert felt a warm glow of pride. "It just popped into my head."

They passed the clearing with the abandoned suitcase. Harri picked it up with an embarrassed look. "Running away wasn't such a great idea," she said.

"I was pretty awful to you," Robert said.

"I don't blame you for hating it when I barged in and changed your life. I bragged about the things I've done, but really I was a little jealous of you."

Robert's jaw dropped open. "Why would you be jealous of me?"

"You have such a nice life. My parents love me, I know that, and I love them, too. But Fred and Margaret *like* you. You make things with your dad, and your mom lets you bake with her. And you have a special place that's just for you. Sometimes I get pretty tired of being away from home so much. . . ." Harri's voice trailed off.

Robert stopped just as they reached the edge of the yard. "I'll share it with you. Then you'll have a special place, too." He was rewarded with a shy smile. Then they had to run and catch up with Monster and the fawn.

"Now what do we do?" asked Harri.

Robert wiped his head with his hand. There had been too many problems for one morning. "We are probably in trouble at school." he said. "And at home. But no matter what, we have to save this baby. It was our fault the mother was killed."

Harri nodded gravely in agreement. "Let's bring her into the kitchen and give her something to eat," she suggested.

Robert hesitated. "What if she goes ... you know what ... in the house?"

"Then we'll clean it up," Harri answered cheerfully.

"All right," said Robert. "But only for a minute. Mom and Dad are going to be mad enough without finding a deer in the kitchen."

The fawn followed them willingly. Her tiny hooves tip-tapped across the polished floors as she investigated the strange new surroundings.

"She's so sweet," Harri said. "What shall we call her? I know—how about Violet?"

Robert nodded. "It fits her. Wouldn't it be wonderful if we could keep her?"

Monster sat on the rug beside the sink. His tail kept a rhythm with the fawn's prancing hooves. "What should we feed her?" Harri asked.

"Milk, I suppose," Robert said. "A deer is a mammal," he continued, remembering his science lessons. "And all mammals drink milk."

"But this is cow's milk," Harri said. She took the carton from the refrigerator and set it on the counter.

"Maybe she needs a different kind of milk. And how are we going to give it to her?"

The fawn was nibbling on the tablecloth. It pulled on the corner, nearly upsetting the napkin holder and salt and pepper shakers. Robert grabbed them just in time. "Here, hold these while I straighten this tablecloth," he said, handing them to Harri. He gently tugged the end of the cloth out of Violet's mouth and positioned it back on the table.

"Hey, where did she go?" Harri said as she arranged the shakers back in the middle of the table.

Monster jumped up and charged toward the hall door that led to the bedrooms. He bumped into Robert, who stumbled backward. Harri grabbed for him, but he sat down hard on the floor, pulling Harri down with him.

"Are you all right?" Harri asked. A grin tugged at the corners of her mouth.

Robert gave a rueful nod. "I guess we look pretty silly."

"I'm sorry I made you miss the Halloween parade," Harri said suddenly. "I know you would have won the prize for the scariest costume."

"Maybe I'll win next year," Robert said.

"I still feel awful about it. And now the deer is dead because of me." The laughter had drained from her face, and she started to cry. "What are we going to do about the fawn?"

Robert scrambled to his feet. For a second he'd almost forgotten. "We'd better get her. Maybe we can put her in the garage until Mom gets home."

96

Harri stood up, too, but before they could move, the back door opened and Mrs. Sylvester stepped into the kitchen. "What on Earth is going on?" she demanded. "And why aren't you two in school?"

FOURTEEN

What Do You Do with a Deer, Dear?

"It's my fault," explained Harri. "I was running away. Because of the spider."

"Spider?" Mrs. Sylvester looked nervously around the kitchen as though she expected to see spiders crawling out of the sink.

"It's a costume," Robert said. "But then the man in the blue car killed the deer."

"And we had to save the fawn," Harri finished the story.

"I still don't understand," Mrs. Sylvester was saying, when from the hallway came a loud *thump! thump!*

"Oh my gosh. She's in my room," Robert yelled. He sprinted down the hall with Harri. Mrs. Sylvester huffed along close behind.

"My goodness," was all Mrs. Sylvester could manage as they all crowded in the doorway.

Violet was on Robert's bed, bouncing up and down with little odd stiff-legged jumps.

"Just like a little kid," Harri said, laughing. She went in and sat on the edge of the bed. Instantly Violet stopped jumping and curled up beside her. She surveyed the room with her large eyes and yawned.

"I think we had better get her out of here," Mrs. Sylvester said. "I called your mother when the school notified me that you were absent. I don't imagine she will be too pleased to find this little fellow in the house."

Together they coaxed the deer outside and into the garage.

"We were going to feed it," Robert explained as they arranged some crates to make a tiny stall. At Mrs. Sylvester's suggestion they lined the bottom with grass and leaves.

"My husband and I raised some calves once," said Mrs. Sylvester. "We mixed them up a formula called milk replacer. People give it to calves because they want to save their mothers' milk for humans. I might still have the bottle we used somewhere."

Mrs. Ott drove up just as Mrs. Sylvester went to look for the bottle. She looked at the fawn while Robert and Harri tried to explain.

"Let's go in the house," she said. "We'll let the fawn rest while I call the sheriff. And then I want to hear the whole story." She pointed to Monster, who was sitting like a guard near the fawn's stall. "Looks like we have a pretty good baby-sitter here."

Robert and Harri sat silently at the kitchen table while Mrs. Ott telephoned the sheriff. She explained what had happened and listened for a minute. Then she jotted down a number and hung up the telephone.

"They will send someone to take care of the mother deer's body," she told them, "but we have to call the game warden ourselves and tell him we have the fawn."

"Why?" Robert wailed. "We want to take care of it."

"It's against the law to let just anyone keep a wild animal," Mrs. Ott said gently. "That's to keep people from making pets out of them."

"Don't you think he might make an exception?" asked Harri. "That fawn would have starved to death if it wasn't for us."

"I don't know," Mrs. Ott admitted. "But even if he did, it would be a big responsibility. And I don't think either one of you has acted very responsibly today." She looked at Harri. "Just where did you think you were going?"

"I didn't really know. Then my suitcase got too heavy and I just sat in the woods."

Robert gave her a grateful look. "It wasn't all Harri's fault," he told his mother. "I told her I hated her and wished she had never come."

"I understand why you were angry about the costume," said Mrs. Ott. "But I think both of you acted very immaturely. Perhaps your father and I will have to reconsider trusting you together without a baby-sitter. And Robert, I still expect you to treat Harri kindly."

Unexpectedly, Harri stamped her foot. "I'm tired of being treated like a guest," she yelled. "I want to be treated like I'm part of this family."

"Hmmm," said Mrs. Ott. "Perhaps we have handled this wrong. We'll talk more about this later. But right now I had better call the game warden."

"Do you think he really might let us keep her?" whispered Robert as Mrs. Ott began to dial.

Harri nodded. "If he doesn't, I will scream," she said mischievously.

Mrs. Sylvester tapped on the door. "I found it," she said, waving a large glass bottle with a nipple screwed onto the end. It looked like a human baby's bottle, only bigger.

"We have to report the fawn to the game warden," said Robert. "He might not let us keep her."

"That's too bad," said Mrs. Sylvester. "But maybe it's for the best. I had a friend once who made a pet of a deer. When hunting season came the deer walked right up to some hunters. They killed it."

Harri suddenly looked embarrassed. "Thanks for helping us. I'm sorry I was so rude that day when Monster got in your yard."

Mrs. Sylvester smiled, and Robert thought it made her look much younger. "I shouldn't have been so grouchy. I can see that Monster is a very special dog. Most dogs would have chased the fawn—or worse."

"The game warden can't come until tomorrow afternoon," said Mrs. Ott, hanging up the telephone. She had been writing something on a piece of paper. "He gave me instructions for making formula for the fawn, but he says milk replacer should work fine."

"Where can we get some?" Robert asked.

"The feed store," his mother answered. "But the game warden told me that fawns in the wild often wait for two days while their mothers are foraging for food.

102

So let's wait until your father comes home and perhaps he will go for the milk replacer."

Mrs. Ott sat down to chat with Mrs. Sylvester at the kitchen table and Robert and Harri went out to sit on the front porch. It was much too late now to think of going to school.

Later that afternoon Sally Anne walked by, her arms full of books.

"What are you doing home so early?" she stopped to ask. Robert and Harri took her to the garage to meet Violet while Robert explained how they got her. He noticed Sally Anne's nails were painted a nice soft shade of pink, and for once she wasn't chewing gum.

"Did you and Jeffrey make up?" he asked, because she looked so happy.

"Who?" She laughed. "Boring. Jeffrey is yesterday's news. My new boyfriend's name is Brian."

When Mr. Ott came home a short time later, the story was told for the fourth time that day. He went to the feed store for the milk replacer, and when he returned Robert and Harri took turns holding Mrs. Sylvester's bottle while Violet slurped the liquid down eagerly. Then they shut the garage for the night, leaving Monster curled up with the fawn, still keeping guard.

Robert was thoughtful during dinner. He didn't even make a face at the beets, though he had decided long ago that any vegetable that was red was not for him. Later he went to his room to write in his journal. So much had happened that day that he filled up two pages. He was still writing when Harri tapped on the door.

103

"Your mother says she can fix the spider suit," Harri said. "At least you can wear it next year."

"It's all right," Robert said honestly. Compared with saving Violet, winning the costume contest no longer seemed important.

Harri picked at a piece of fuzz on Robert's bed. "What if we make friends with the fawn and she gets killed, like the deer Mrs. Sylvester's friend had?"

Robert thought about this. "Let's worry about that later," he said. "First we have to see if the warden will let us keep her."

FIFTEEN

The P.T.W.A.C.

"Some kid in the fifth grade won the prize for the overall best costume," Scott said the next morning. "He was a robot."

"But who do you think won the scariest?" Jason asked. From the grin across his face it wasn't hard to guess. "Your Dracula costume looked great! I splashed catsup all over the front of my shirt. It looked like I had just drunk someone's blood."

"Why didn't you two come to school yesterday?" Scott asked. "You missed all the fun."

Harri looked at Robert and they both laughed. "We didn't miss any fun," Harri said. Together they told the story of the fawn.

"Wow," said Scott. "Do you think the game warden will let you keep the fawn?"

"Cross your fingers for us," Robert said. Harri was unusually silent, and Robert looked at her. "You still want to keep Violet, don't you?"

"Of course," she said. She looked at the ground.

"What's wrong with Harri?" Jason asked after Harri left to tell Mandy and Jennifer about the fawn.

"I don't know," Robert answered. "I guess she's worried that we might not be able to keep her."

"How come you two are friends all of a sudden?" asked Scott. "I thought you hated each other."

"She's not so bad when you get to know her," Robert said.

"Do you think you guys will ever race again?" Jason asked as the bell rang.

Harri was standing close enough to hear, and Robert saw that she was listening for his answer.

Robert thought for a minute. "Sure. We'll all race again, but only if Harri promises not to let me win." He saw her smile. "When I beat you I want to know it's for real," he continued.

"Agreed," said Harri. Scott and Jason shrugged at each other in amazement.

They trooped into the school together just as the bell rang to start the day. Mr. Cross was waiting by the door. "I hear you two had quite an adventure yesterday," he said. "Would you like to tell the class about it?"

When everyone was settled, Robert and Harri stood in front of the class and told them about Violet. Everyone laughed when they told about the fawn bouncing on the bed.

"Has anyone else had an experience with wild animals?" Mr. Cross asked when they had finished.

"We found a baby rabbit once, but it died," said Kirstin.

"My aunt had a pet raccoon," volunteered Brad. "It was real cute when it was little, but when it got older it was kind of mean and it killed their parakeet. They had to turn it loose."

"Wild animals are wonderful," said Mr. Cross. "But generally speaking they do not do well in captivity. There are many interesting careers working with wild animals. Perhaps that will be something we can discuss another time. Right now let's take out our math books and turn to page forty-nine."

Robert groaned quietly. Fractions were one of his least favorite things and it was difficult to concentrate. He kept thinking about what Mr. Cross had said. He hadn't been looking at Robert when he spoke, but nevertheless Robert felt that the words were meant for him. He thought of Violet and the funny way she had sucked on the bottle when he'd fed her that morning. When she was done she had nuzzled him softly. He loved her already.

"We're going to race again," Scott yelled when the bell rang.

Several children clapped. Robert realized they had missed watching the daily race as much as he had missed running it. Mr. Cross went with them to the playground. "I think I will speak to the principal," he said thoughtfully. "Even if we don't have a track team maybe we can have some sort of competition with the other grade schools."

"Isn't it funny that Robert and Harri should both be such good runners?" Jason asked.

"Not so strange," said Mr. Cross. "We all inherit certain things from our parents. I'll bet somewhere back in Harri and Robert's family tree someone else loved to run. Those kinds of things are carried in our genes. Genes are like a set of instructions for making us, and Robert and Harri share some of the same instructions."

Scott, Jason, Robert, and Harri lined up against the school building wall.

"On your mark, get set, GO," the watching children chanted.

They were off. Robert and Harri ran neck and neck, pounding feet keeping perfect time together. Robert held himself back, saving some energy for a final burst of speed at the end. The wind howled past his ears, blending with the children's excited screams. The fence was there, and he touched it, whirling around in a fast return. He was running better than he ever had; he was an eagle, soaring free over the clouds. Then the sound of pounding feet brought him back to Earth and he knew that Harri was still right beside him. She was grinning . . . no, she was laughing. For a minute he felt the old anger, until he realized that she wasn't looking at him. At the same instant he realized the pounding feet he'd heard were on the other side of him, and Scott flew by and touched the wall a split second ahead of him.

The playground erupted in pandemonium. Every-one was laughing and cheering, and Scott's proud smile stretched from ear to ear.

"You've been practicing," Harri gasped, through her laughter. "Robbie and I were so busy trying to beat each other, we forgot about you."

"I'm going to do it, too, one of these days," Jason said cheerfully.

Robert laughed, too. He wondered how a person could lose a race and still feel so good. He didn't even bother to remind Harri not to call him Robbie.

They were all still excited when they walked back into the school, but the rest of the day dragged by slowly as Robert worried about the game warden's visit.

At last the final bell rang. Harri didn't wait for Jennifer and Mandy. She and Robert hurried home together, eager to spend some time with Violet. Mrs. Sylvester had agreed to keep an eye on the fawn until the family got home. She was just leaving the garage when Robert and Harri walked up the drive. Monster ran out to greet them, but as soon as they'd both scratched his big ears he ran back to his place by the fawn.

Robert noticed Mrs. Sylvester was holding a package.

"I did the silliest thing," Mrs. Sylvester said, holding out the package. "Do you remember when I showed you my father's model ships? It made me think I would like to try to make one myself. So I bought this kit. But my old hands are so shaky, I can't imagine what ever possessed me to think I could. Then I remembered that you were saving for a kit and I thought you might be interested."

Robert had forgotten all about the ship-in-a-bottle

kit. He looked into the box. It was just the one he had saved all summer to buy.

"Hey, the box isn't even opened," he said.

Mrs. Sylvester seemed embarrassed. "No, it isn't. Now I want you to show me when you finish." She gave a cheery wave and started back to her house.

Suddenly Robert did something that amazed even him. He ran right up to Mrs. Sylvester and hugged his arms around her ample waist.

Mrs. Sylvester looked surprised and Robert thought he saw tears in her eyes. But she blinked them back and smiled. "Remember, I want to see you finish it."

"I will," he promised. He turned and walked slowly back to the garage. It was strange. The two people in his life he had disliked the most were turning out to be the nicest of all. They had certainly changed. Then a thought struck him. Maybe he was the one who had changed.

"I'll bet she bought it just for you," Harri said, admiring the picture on the box.

Robert nodded. "Would you like to help me make it?" he offered.

"Nah," said Harri, waving her hand. "I'm not very good at models. All those tiny pieces. Ugh."

They were looking at Violet when Mrs. Ott pulled into the driveway. Right behind her was a green pickup with a round emblem on the door. "He's here," Robert said. His stomach did a strange little flip-flop.

Robert watched his mother introduce herself to the game warden, and the two of them walked to the garage.

The game warden looked at Violet. "That's a fine little baby," he said, stroking her head.

"This is Mr. Ames," said Robert's mother. "And this is Robert and Harri. They are the ones who found the fawn."

Mr. Ames had a broad pleasant face with leathery wrinkles, as though he spent a lot of time in the sun. His smile was warm, and Robert felt hopeful. Mr. Ames seemed friendly and nice.

But in the next instant his hopes were dashed. "You know I have to take the fawn," he said gently, pulling out a leather leash from his pocket. "Don't worry. We'll take good care of her, and as soon as she's old enough we will release her back to the wild."

"We could take care of her," Robert pleaded. "We'd do just what you tell us to do." He looked at Harri for support, but she was strangely silent.

Mr. Ames had a serious look on his face. "The law was made for a reason. Well-meaning people like you take fawns out of the woods, thinking the mothers have abandoned them. But as I told your mother, does sometimes leave their babies for several days while they feed."

Mr. Ott had arrived while they were talking. "I don't think you understand," he said. "The children saw the mother deer get hit by a car. We are sure it is an orphan."

"That's different, then," said Mr. Ames. "But you would be surprised how often people think they are rescuing a fawn, when they are really taking it from its mother. But the problem remains the same. The deer

111

must be released, and that will be very difficult if you have grown fond of it. And it's even more serious if the fawn is attached to you."

"I would be willing to supervise the project," Mr. Ott said with a look at Robert. "I admit I don't know much about deer, but you could leave us instructions, and check as often as you like."

Robert held his breath. Mr. Ames really seemed to be considering the idea. Then Harri spoke for the first time.

"No, don't give in. We would get attached to the fawn. Every time we fed it we would pet it and play with it. We couldn't help it." She gave Robert a helpless look. "Remember what Mrs. Sylvester said about her friend's deer? That's what would happen to Violet. Or she would be killed by a dog because she's not afraid of Monster."

Hearing his name, Monster stood up and whined softly. The fawn looked with trust at the big dog and rubbed her head on his. Robert didn't wait to hear any more. He ran from the garage, hot tears filling his eyes. He raced to the plum tree and climbed up, shivering a little because of the frosty air. Most of the leaves had already fallen and he could see clearly as Mr. Ames led Violet to the truck and locked her in a wire cage in the back.

Mr. Ott started for the plum tree, but Harri said something and he turned back to the house. Robert watched Harri walk to the tree. She stood underneath and looked up.

"I suppose you hate me again."

Robert shook his head and sighed. "No, you were right. I knew it all the time, but I just couldn't say it."

"Can I come up?" Harri asked.

When Robert nodded she climbed up and sat on the branch. "Remember the first day I came?" she asked after a minute.

Robert smiled in spite of his sorrow. "I guess I really looked dumb."

Harri giggled. "You did, but that's not what I meant. I was talking about the F.G.O. Club. I've been thinking about it. Jennifer and Mandy are nice, but just talking about clothes and stuff gets kind of boring. How about if we had a club that really did something?"

"Like what?"

"Maybe we could study about wild animals. Find out what we could do to really help. Like your father making bluebird houses."

"We could meet here in the tree," Robert said, warming to the idea. "We could call it the P.T.W.A.C."

"The Plum Tree Wild Animal Club," Harri guessed. "I'll bet a lot of kids would be interested. You could be president," she offered. "After all, it is your plum tree."

Robert smiled. "It's our plum tree. And maybe we could draw straws to see who is president. Or take turns."

"For our first project you could write a story about Violet and I'll draw the pictures. That way we'll never forget her," Harri said as they walked back to the house.

Mr. and Mrs. Ott were waiting when they walked in

113

the door. Mrs. Ott gave Robert a sympathetic look, but he smiled at them reassuringly.

"Guess what, Fred," Harri said. "We're going to make a club to study wild animals."

Mr. Ott looked stern. "You are not making anything until your room is clean, do you understand? And furthermore, from now on I am Uncle Fred, and this is Aunt Margaret."

Harri's face got red, and for a minute Robert thought she would say something angry. Instead she smiled. "I'll clean it right this minute, Uncle Fred."

Mr. Ott chuckled. "That's the first time I ever made someone happy by giving them work to do. How about you, Robert? Would you like a job to cheer you up?" he teased.

"No thanks," Robert said cheerfully. "But while we're changing names, how about calling me Robbie?"

"Sure thing, Robbie," Mr. Ott said, trying it out. "But why?"

"Well, for one thing it sounds friendlier. And sometimes a little change is good for you," Robert said.